THE WEDDING DJ'S DIARY

THE WEDDING DJ'S DIARY

CHRISTOPHER BARTNESS

Published by Outland Sound

Contact: outlandsound@yahoo.com

Website: christopherbartness.com

*Hardback version available upon request.

To My Loving Family

TABLE OF
CONTENTS

INTRODUCTION

FUNDAMENTAL TO WRITING *The Wedding DJ's Diary* is the author's experience as a wedding DJ for over twenty years. His reflections on the actual personalities and events are hindsight intertwined with introspection of someone older and hopefully wiser. Sometimes we must look to the past to truly appreciate the present. His prose is tainted by the romantic tendency to remember what may have been as opposed to what was. The funniest and most disturbing bits are all true. Memories forgotten or faded have been embellished with nostalgia.

PLAY THAT FUNKY MUSIC, WHITE BOY

GROWING UP I was only frightened of one thing: getting killed by Bigfoot. Through the late 1960s and early '70s there were weekly reports of Bigfoot sightings in the area. An older boy named Tommy lived next door. He had the only stepdad in the neighborhood. Tommy would often tell us stories about the Bigfoots; yes, there was more than one, according to him. And they were randomly attacking people in their cars. After catching the speeding vehicle, the Bigfoots would grab the occupants by the neck and repeatedly bash their heads through the windshield. Those teenagers who chose to park and make out were the easiest prey.

At age five, I pictured the latest victims smooching in their 1965 GT Mustang Fastback, then being beset by Bigfoots. Apparently the 271-horsepower, V-8 engine and four-speed racing transmission were no match in outrunning nine-foot-tall missing links set on homicide. I had to close my eyes and plug my ears as Tommy graphically reenacted the encounter, including sound effects. Apparently, those victims with soft heads needed three or four good bashings in order to breach the glass.

In hindsight, considering that a lot of cars in the late 1960s didn't have seatbelts to begin with (and that most people refused to wear them), one could find countless cases of people's heads and bodies being bashed through windshields. The police reports may have cited alcohol or excessive speeds, but at age five, I knew the truth: death by Bigfoot.

As I got older, I dismissed the whole Bigfoot thing. By age sixteen I knew nothing could outrun a 1965 GT Mustang Fastback, including a police cruiser. Trust me.

Dropping the Bigfoot anxiety was easy. Overcoming my cravings and enslavement to PEZ was another matter. At the height of my addiction, I was six years old and had collected fifty PEZ dispensers. I was consuming sixty sugary pellets per day. It didn't matter the flavor or the personification of the dispenser, all I lived for was lifting the head of the iconic character, activating the spring, and receiving my sweet fix. Intervention came in the form of a lengthy visit with my dentist.

He was a sorcerer, this one. He could tell at a glance the violated, unholy, soiled mouth of a child who had been dabbling in PEZ. Oh yes, when boys played with PEZ, they needed to pay for their confectionary sins. The dental drill was the harbinger of justice. Just enough Novocaine to let you think you were numb. When you cried out, he called you a wuss and slapped you across your seminumb face and just kept drilling. After receiving my second mercury filling, I wet my pants.

Upon arriving home, I immediately threw out all my PEZ dispensers. My most prized, go-to PEZ addiction rigs that helped me chase the dragon and ride the horse were set afire. I expressed my new sobriety by dripping their poisonous plastic on the ant hills in my backyard. Two of the PEZ dispensers were Sid And Marty Krofft originals of *H.R. Pufnstuf* and *the Bugaloos*. I also had a

Marsha Brady. If I had even one of those today, I would never have to work again.

We had a single AM radio in my house growing up. No stereo, only a mono record player from JCPenney. My parents owned no records. I did have several LP records of Disney movies that I could play while following along with an abridged story booklet. I had *Bambi*, *Cinderella*, *Dumbo*, and *Pinocchio*. The latter two were less traumatic than the actual movies I saw in 1970 on a double bill at the 112th Street drive-in.

I visited Disneyland at age fifty. It's a truly magical place. But there is a dark presence there. I saw it foreshadowed in the Disney movies I watched at the drive-in growing up. There are elements about Disney that channel both sides of the force—the light and the dark—like the Jedi. The fact that they bought the Star Wars franchise was the final proof I needed. Trust me, it's there. Mr. Disney's desk remains the same as he left it in 1966. They say if the light is on in Mr. Disney's office, he's there, still working. I say his ghost is everywhere in the park, and it creeps me out. They froze his head. But what of the spirit?

My early musical influences came from watching *Hee Haw* reruns on the local television station. I started watching the show knowing that following its speedy credits, *Star Trek* would be on, so I could finally see my Asian friend, Sulu, and the photon torpedoes. From age two to seven, Roy Clark, Buck Owens and the whole *Hee Haw* gang were the entirety of my musical world. I later learned that the music on *Hee Haw* was called "square."

I remember watching a Christmas special on late-night TV when I was five. My parents were having friends over, so I was allowed to stay up past my usual bedtime. We kids called their friends "uncle" and "aunt," although we had no blood relation to either couple. Up to age ten I had no idea who any of my blood relations really were. Calling everyone aunt and uncle was just a middle-class affectation, similar to all the hippies calling each other brother, sister, or man.

On the television Christmas special, a black performer, I believe it was Ella Fitzgerald, was singing her version of "The Little Drummer Boy." The first verse was very melodious and similar to the way we sang it in church. Ella went rogue on the second verse, though, taking great liberty with the meter and melody. No longer was it the song I'd grown up with. Now it was drummer Tony Williams spitting out three-against-four grooves as Charles Mingus climbed the beanstalk on his upright bass to visit *Alice in Wonderland* to lay some skin on Chick Chorea about the *Straight, No Chaser* shit he was laying down to Miles Davis about the *Stella by Starlight* birth of Jesus.

After hearing Ella's rendition, my fake-aunt Dorthy pronounced it sacrilegious discord. She preferred the way the children in church would sing it. You know, traditional.

I don't know what *traditional* meant to Aunt Dorthy, but I have vivid recollections of my first-grade Sunday school class singing off-key. Often the accompaniment would include giggling, burping, the occasional fart, followed by an "ooh, that stinks," and climaxing in a refrain of "he who smelt it, dealt it."

To my five-year-old ears I thought Ella was a great singer. She was just singing the wrong notes like a lot of jazz musicians did. Ella only needed a little musical guidance. If Roy Clark, Buck Owens, and the whole *Hee Haw* gang had been there to help, all would have been well in my holiday world. Ho, ho, ho!

People didn't dance on *Hee Haw* so much as sit around singing and clapping. Occasionally they tapped their feet on the chorus. These were the formative years for me. A bunch of white people playing the same country music in syndication forever and ever, amen. Occasionally I would hear the Hager Twins sing something more contemporary. Their cover of "Black and White" made famous by *Three Dog Night* was groundbreaking for the show. This song wasn't so square. Who knew?

Growing up, I was often alone. And as anyone knows, a child left forsaken will begin to experiment. Without parental supervision, or direction, any impressionable youth may turn to questionable outside influences and be corrupted.

I began watching *Soul Train* when I was six. It was 1971 when the disco inferno was just beginning its pyre. This was real music with real horns and musicians and "dancing." All this before "the Man" and all the corporate people started cashing in. By the late seventies, the mainstream community was trying to steal the soul out of soul music with even white groups from England cashing in with their interpretations of early disco standards using high falsettos. White groups were covering songs by the Tavares, the O'Jays, and the Trammps. The soul train was sadly going off its rails and becoming the money train.

In the early years of *Soul Train* the dancing was a celebration of good times and better times yet to come. It was always joyful and full of promise, a lot like gospel music. The *Soul Train* music had what I later learned was called "groove." It wasn't square like the music on *Hee Haw*. The dancers on *Soul Train* were free and not afraid to take chances, wave their arms, shake their butts. The men would wear six-inch platform shoes and what looked to be my older sister's sequined blouses unbuttoned to the naval with a gold chain around their necks.

The first episode had host Don Cornelius introduce the first-ever Soul Train dance line in a kind of dance off to "Jungle Boogie." It was spontaneous and live and almost exclusively black. Later, Dick Clark from *American Bandstand* would create *Soul Unlimited* to be a direct competitor for the soul of *Soul Train*. This poor attempt at cashing in on the black market by the Man was even condemned by Reverend Jesse Jackson. He got the show canceled due to what Jesse called "the presence of overly pronounced racial overtones." I think Jesse just wanted to keep the cream out of the coffee.

After watching my first episode of *Soul Train*, I wanted to dance. After moving the living-room furniture, I created my own dance line. Looking into the pretend camera on the piano, I would dance down the runway just like the dudes on *Soul Train*. Tucking my socks into my pants like knickers, I borrowed my older sister's sequined blouse and unbuttoned it to my navel. After adding my mother's gold chain, I believed I had soul.

After retrieving my parents' AM radio from the kitchen, I was ready. "Mama's Pearl" by the Jackson Five was playing on one of the pop stations, and I cranked the volume. My dance routine began by doing the robot. Although my version looked more like the vacuum cleaner than the robot. After a soul vaccination, I sashayed back to try all over again. My moves this time included blindingly fast hip thrusts to the left and right. I then jumped from the couch to my dad's recliner, rebounding off the coffee table to end in the splits shredding my Sears Toughskins jeans and popping two buttons off my sister's blouse.

Mrs. Durkey walked her dog every day at three thirty. She was very nearsighted. She often stopped in front of our house so her dog could take a pee on my father's prize-winning roses. It was three thirty. As her dog was lifting its leg, Mrs. Durkey looked up to see my over-the-top dancing and unusual outfit through our living-room window. Apparently, I made quite the impression. Mrs. Durkey called my parents later that evening on our rotary phone informing them that I had been cross-dressing and practicing self-abuse.

My parents, being products of post-1930s depression in the Midwest, just sent me to bed an hour early without saying anything. My mother would later pray for me along with her women's group at church about exorcising my confusing behavior. The next day my father signed me up for peewee football and made me give up that new sissy sport called soccer.

My first dance outside our house occurred a year later in the musty-smelling basement of an Eagles Hall. Shortly after the wedding reception began my brother and I ventured upstairs. We opened the door and stepped into a dark room with lots of people smoking cigarettes. There were neon beer signs, a jukebox, and pull-tab machines. In the background, I could hear Buck Owens singing "Act Naturally." And that's what me and my brother did.

We sat ourselves at the smoky bar and yelled for the bartender to pour us a drink. Just like they did on *Gunsmoke*. The patrons at the bar burst into laughter at the novelty of two children walking into a bar and demanding a drink. My brother and I were incorrigible.

The bartender, Glenda, played along with us as the crowd of mostly men fell in behind us. Using her best country drawl, she said, "What will you have, cowboy?" My brother shouted whiskey to the infectious laughter of all. I countered with an "on the rocks," remembering an episode of *M*A*S*H*. Unabashed laughter ensued. The Smothers Brother had nothing on my brother and me.

Glenda quickly filled two water glasses with coke from a soda gun and slid them down the bar. We pounded our drinks and slammed the glasses upside down. The patrons rewarded us once again with hallowed laughter and praise. A man standing behind us yelled, "Give the boys a real drink." Glenda appeared amused but felt that the joke had gone far enough. The children would have to leave. She was beginning to usher us toward the basement door, then stopped. A table of five had walked in and were waiting to be seated.

After she left, a one-armed man wearing a VFW hat asked if we wanted to have a real drink. My brother and I nodded. He took two empty glasses from the bar and filled them halfway with a clear liquid smelling like the juniper bushes in our backyard. Taking the soda gun from the counter, he topped off our glasses with some fizzy stuff. The man told us it was a gin and tonic. My brother and I pounded our drinks, per previous cue, and set the glasses back on the bar. Glenda came back and escorted us to the basement. My parents hadn't even noticed we were gone.

A gin and tonic tasted a lot like 7UP mixed with cough syrup. No matter, I liked anything fizzy. Minutes later, I began to feel warm and a kind of happy I'd never experienced before. A few minutes after that, I was talking to the potato salad. Looking over, I saw my brother chattering away with the prime rib about the pros and cons of nuclear power. The Caesar salad remained indifferent. I didn't know what a gin and tonic was, but I liked it. And then I heard the music.

It wasn't a *Soul Train* artist like the O'Jays or the Spinners, and it wasn't *Hee Haw* either. It was Creedence Clearwater Revival. The cover band hired for the reception had just kicked off with "Travelin' Band." There was no disco ball or gold chains, but there was the intoxicating beat of the music. I felt the presence of Saint Vitus, the patron saint of dance himself, within me. Like Fezziwig, a character out of *A Christmas Carol*, I was loose of limb and dexterous in every fiber. Like a young Michael Jackson, I was a dancing machine.

My brother also tried to dance, opting for a dervish type of spin dance. It was obvious he had never watched *Soul Train*. Looking more like an Olympic skater than a dancer, he was trying to lift one leg over his head. He continued to spin until dizzily banging his head on the banquet table holding the prime rib. I guess we know who won that argument. He was carried to a folding chair by the catering staff.

In the middle of the dance floor I was grooving out my version of the Bus Stop. Glancing over I noticed the look on my mother's face to be that of *please stop*! I just winked at her and continued to dance. This papa opened his brand-new bag, as well as a few others. I tried to replicate all the *Soul Train* choreography from season one into a solo dance-line extravaganza. Opening a huge can of whoop ass, I brought out my "lawn mower" and chased the "funky chicken."

But all good dance lines come to an end. After the band had finished their first song, my parents thought it best for our family to leave. My brother was passed out on a folding chair. Mom was clearly hoping to avoid an incident like the one in the front window with Mrs. Durkey. My father was ready to sign the enlistment papers for the local military academy.

On the drive home I crashed. Being a Saturday evening, church and Sunday school were mere hours away. How could I sing "This Little Gospel Light of Mine" or "Jesus Loves Me" on Sunday morning after defiling myself with demon gin?

Lit up like a neon sign at the Eagles Hall, I continued to buzz until closing. Before last call, it occurred to me that my parents thought my dancing was queer. So I must be queer. This was the real reason for all the encouragement to play football and be a Green Beret. After all, how could anyone play the manly game of football or defeat communism and be queer? I had played smear the queer before, but that meant tackling anyone who had the football. Most of my playmates would pass the ball before they were tackled to make someone else the queer. I remember playing with my best friend, Byron Jones. He routinely kept the ball and appeared to enjoy being tackled.

Before losing consciousness, I realized that the guys

on *Soul Train* had figured out a way to dance that didn't make you look queer, so nobody would tackle you or send you to military school. The *Soul Train* guys had the right balance between blouses and football. Spiraling into inebriated sleep came the final epiphany: watching *Hee Haw* had been a complete waste of time.

The next morning I woke feeling like a Bigfoot had bashed my head through a windshield over and over. For the next few years, I played football and quit dancing. I was cured.

When I first began DJing in my late twenties, I knew three things for sure. One, my chance of getting attacked by a Bigfoot was unlikely. Two, I was only a fair dancer, despite the early funk infusions from *Soul Train*. And three, those who can't do, teach. While it was true that my early musical influences came from watching reruns of *Hee Haw*, there were still some country songs that made me want to dance. Although the music on *Soul Train* wasn't so square overall, there were still songs that only sort of made you want to dance. Regardless of genre, I could listen to any tune and determine whether a song was danceable or not to the masses. I use this standard even to this day when selecting dance music for any event.

My second public celebration of dance took place in junior high. My partner was the exotic French student named Monique. At the movies a week before she taught me that French was also a type of kiss. Oui, oui. I danced the Bump, she humped, and we tripped the light fantastic to Andy Gibb's "Shadow Dancing." In the middle of our dance Monique was asked to leave by the vice principal due to her lewd and oversexualized behavior. Monique had to borrow a quarter from Mr. Tibbs to call her father on the cafeteria payphone. I was allowed back into the dance only after a cautionary reminder about school spirit and appropriate conduct.

After returning, I noticed all the boys standing on the left side of the cafeteria and girls standing to the right. The recent intervention by Mr. Tibbs had apparently killed the vibe. There were only two couples dancing as "Give It to Me Baby" by Rick James was winding down. My Asian friend, Patrick, told me the two couples dancing were doing it for real. I still wasn't really sure what "doing it" was, despite taking three years of sex education. But I thought I'd like it.

The DJ switched it up and put on a slow song, "How Deep Is Your Love" by the Bee Gees. Slowly, both sides of the room began to merge. I spied Julie Morgan from my home economics class. We were in the same baking group, and she always looked great in her James Jeans. When she scrambled her eggs there were never any pieces of shell.

Earlier in the week we'd accidentally touched bottoms while squeezing between workstations, buttering our scones. I made my move, pushing past a very disappointed Byron Jones. I tapped Julie on the shoulder and asked her to dance. She agreed. As we made our way to the dance floor I could tell she was wearing Love's Baby Soft perfume. Mmm.

I remember seeing one of the commercials for Love's Baby Soft in the early 1970s. The thirty-second commercial showed a grown woman dressed like a little girl staring vacantly into the camera while licking a lollipop. The narrator explained how she'd started as a baby and about how innocence was just so sexy. It was reminiscent of the movie trailer for *Rosemary's Baby* I'd seen the week before. Nobody needed to tell me what sexy was—Julie Morgan wearing James Jeans and buttering scones. Ooh la la.

I placed my hands on her shoulders the way you check the pads on a fellow football player. We kept the mandated six inches between us according to the school conduct manual. Her hair was beautifully feathered, body doused in perfume. I was wearing the Old Spice aftershave my fake uncle had given me for Christmas. As we danced our bouquets intertwined. Years away, I envisioned myself stepping off a maritime schooner and ravishing the woman I loved after she left work at the PEZ factory. Just like in the days of old.

After several titillating moments, I leaned in. We were touching foreheads. As the second verse started, I realized that dancing with Julie Morgan felt a lot like drinking a gin and tonic. By the chorus, my palms were sweating, soaking the padded shoulders of her dress. She looked up to meet my gaze, our foreheads sweaty. She smiled. This was my moment to teach Julie Morgan that French was more than a language. I leaned in for the kiss. The tips of our tongues would gently touch, propelled by the growing desire inside each of us to be as one. I closed my eyes. My mouth came forward, only to lick the back of Mr. Tibbs's hand.

I was kicked out of the dance for good. Mr. Tibbs lent me a quarter so I could call my mother to pick me up. Later that evening, Mr. Tibbs called our house. He felt morally obligated to inform my parents about how twisted their youngest son really was. Mr. Tibbs also told them that he wouldn't be surprised if my fetish for hand licking didn't turn into something even more perverted, like self-abuse in front of the living-room window while cross-dressing. Or worse. What if I became a communist?

After relaying my version of the dance, my parents seemed relieved. They weren't happy with my inappropriate licking but were happy that I'd been dancing with girls; yes, plural.

I was still sent to my room an hour early. Lying on my bed, I thought about Monique and some other girls I'd seen at the dance. Closing my eyes, I tried to relive my near-kissing experience with Julie Morgan. I wondered, was she really baby soft?

THE CHICKEN BONE

THE WEDDING RECEPTION was in a warehouse. Not the white church or Eagles Hall I grew up knowing as the usual destination for local weddings, events, and parties. Oh, how I loved going to the Eagles Hall for wedding receptions as a boy. They'd usually be in the musty-smelling reception room located in the basement. My brother and I would venture upstairs to the dark, smoky bar and solicit drinks from old men wearing funny hats. Or maybe that was the Elks Club? Anyway, by age ten my brother and I were convinced that a gin and tonic was nature's perfect food. It was magical.

This was not the kind of warehouse you see on reruns of *The Office* with modern conveniences, such as elevators and coffeepots, or lovable personalities driving around on forklifts. This warehouse was more like the cruel counting house from Dickens's *A Christmas Carol*. It was constructed around the same time as the story, in 1850, and much like the Ghost of Christmas Present it had aged rapidly and poorly.

The location was in the downtown at the height of the now infamous Artist Loft Relocation of the early 1990s. For those now smoking legal marijuana, let me refresh your long-departed memory. The art community was thriving, and any building that was condemned was in vogue and worthy of habitation, if not plain old-fashioned squatting. Most of these loft spaces were just a match away from becoming a new condominium or parking lot.

Artists, so-called and otherwise, flocked to these newly converted spaces in order to live and create. Starving artists, they may have been, but homeless? Never. The local socialists and county and city governments combined forces, assisting enthusiastically in this Renaissance.

Community leaders were desperate and willing to resort to any measure necessary to get miles of easels and disturbing paintings and sculptures off the main streets. Concerned about declining city revenues, the chamber of commerce exerted its full authority. They believed the art community was scaring tourists away from the waterfront market. These important patrons were interested in buying fresh salmon and vegetables, not grotesque art abstractions. Something had to be done.

In the mayor's conservative mind, if someone was going to paint with urine and feces, they might as well do it in the privacy of a loft. Nice move, mayor, you not only succeeded in getting reelected but also in reducing both homelessness and public urination.

Having visited more than a few of these "lofty" studios and having reluctantly experienced the art scene at this time, I'm inclined to view this Renaissance of creativity as Section 8 housing for people seeking to get high and pursue unemployment as a vocation.

It was not the art mecca or the resurgence of the downtown it was trumped up to be in the local media. Shit in, shit out. Had I been able to obtain a loft space,

I may well have begun a career as an artist. My medium would have been full self-expression through nude body painting.

A wedding today is a very personal expression of a couple's love for each other. In the early 1990s it was a political conundrum. At that time, the term "marriage" conjured up only one ideal: one man, one woman standing before an ordained minister, not one of those imposters from the Universalist Church. For shame.

These events required family, friends, the catering staff, and good old Uncle David to wear clothes that induced sweating. Lots of sweating. The bridesmaids' dresses were usually strapless, ill-fitting, and dyed the color of nightshade vegetables.

Enlightened straight couples were sensitive during that time. So as not to flaunt their matrimonial rights or aspirations or offend their same-sex neighbors, straight couples began downplaying their wedding day. A celebration it was, but there was no need to feel too proud while others continued in their civil-union suffrage.

Indeed, overly concerned straight couples began whispering their vows, no longer publicly proclaiming their heterosexuality with loud or raucous "I dos." I witnessed politically correct straight couples during the mid-'90s exchanging vows somberly and apologizing to their gay friends after the wedding.

But the biggest change was to the wedding invitations. No longer were couples sending out bold declarations with ornate embossments and lace. No. Contemporary etiquette was to send invitations the size of a stamp, along with an apology for having the right to marry.

Straight couples should have stood their ground while

remaining sympathetic to their gay brothers and sisters' plight of civil union. If I've learned anything from the LGBTQ community, it's that you must have Pride, and on occasion a parade with drag queens and women riding motorcycles.

Those couples wishing to push the envelope, pun intended, would send out business-card-sized invitations. Sadly, these invitations were still too small to be processed at the post office. Judging by all the no-shows at most wedding receptions, I fear that many wedding announcements just jammed the postal sorting machines.

I sat outside the wedding venue looking at an invitation the size of a tea bag. I double-checked the address. What a ruin.

It was the old steelworks my father had taken me to as a kid. We'd venture out here several times a year to pick up ornately twisted flat bar for fencing projects in the neighborhood. Dad got the pleasure of my company, and I got a milkshake. Win-win. It closed when I was ten.

The building hadn't changed in a quarter of a century. This was a place to shoot heroin, or maybe rats with your .22, not a place to celebrate a wedding. At least the broken windows from forty years ago had been replaced. They now glimmered in the midday overcast like a rainbow in an oil spill. The wooden sliding warehouse panel had been replaced with two black solid-metal fire doors. Grim.

Inside, the décor was Bohemian Bauhaus. I can handle straightforward simplicity, but no paint, no carpet? In the corner, where the sixteen-ton metal press once loomed, only a hole and what looked like a bloodstain the size of a living-room carpet remained. My father had told me numerous times to stay away from "the old widow-maker," as the hydraulic press was called. "If you get caught under the old widow-maker when it comes down, not even God can save you," my father would warn.

I took a moment of silence to honor what remained of that fallen metalworker. Sixteen tons, and what did he get?

The smell? Old-man beer farts piped through gear oil. The old foundry had become the kitchen. The wooden floor was the same, only now with a sticky finish from months of overflowing beer kegs.

Prophetically, the sounds of Alice in Chains murmured from a small FM radio in the kitchen like the Ghost of Metalworks Past. This 150-year-old, 426 max-occupancy rental had, for better or worse, been resurrected.

I unloaded my equipment in thirty minutes and had tunes going an hour before the reception. Kegs of beer were being hauled in along with cases of wine. Tables were decorated, and the cake arrived shortly thereafter. The caterers were putting out hotplates for the buffet, and several trays of appetizers were making the rounds. The reception was set to begin as soon as the couple finished with their wedding photos. The maid of honor would give a signal when the betrothed were arriving, then I was supposed to announce them. Simple.

The happy couple had invited me to DJ their wedding after we met while wine tasting six months prior. Or, more accurately, I was tasting; they were drinking wine out of water glasses.

For our initial meeting, we chose a coffee shop downtown, not a wine bar. They were so cute. They came in holding hands and had that glow about them that only unmarried couples have. The loving and relaxed expressions on their faces told me two things. First, they'd had coitus less than an hour before, both reaching climax. Second, no kids. Although the former exemplifies the obvious latter. We ordered coffee.

This couple was ready, or, should I say, the bride was ready. She produced a scrapbook the size of a large pizza box and thrice as thick. It was filled with several thousand wedding-ceremony agendas and announcements. Then she opened a second pizza box. It contained an equivalent mass of music lists.

I made the joke that somebody had been thinking about "her" special day for quite a while. The bride looked at me deadpan and sent her fiancé to the car for the next set of encyclopizzias. We finally settled on a rough draft after six hours of negotiation. This was followed by a lengthy email exchange which, if printed, could have easily filled another pizza box.

The irony was that by the time we finished planning her unique, one-of-kind, just-our-own, signifies-our-love, share-our-special-day wedding agenda, I could easily have pirated the agenda from the wedding I'd DJ'd a week earlier, changed a few names, and saved us all a lot of time.

I guess sometimes it's all about the journey. Anyway, now we had a "one-of-a-kind" agenda for their special day.

Most brides insist, no, require that her groom be part of the wedding-planning committee. Their rationale is sound. We're a team now and need to start acting like one. The logic follows that if the couple can successfully pull off their own wedding, then a mortgage and children are all future challenges they can overcome. After being involved in the planning of over five hundred weddings, I can attest that raising children isn't that tough. As for a mortgage? My wife and I got our last one online sitting at home in our underwear. No sweat.

Most brides have been thinking about their wedding day for decades before they even meet Mr. Right, or, in some cases, Ms. Right. Some have prewritten scripts where all they need to do is add the groom's name. So, for a fiancé to "groom up" six months before the wedding, it's the equivalent of taking a nearsighted five-year-old T-ball player and starting them against the Yankees in the World Series. Straight to the majors, do not pass go. Trust me, guys, the brides are way out of your league.

After dismissing most of the groom's ideas, the bride then begins to pursue a strategy of totalitarianism. This isn't a democratic process. Usually the groom is assigned one or two simple tasks, such as selecting the type of beer for the reception; occasionally she allows him to choose the band or, in my case, the DJ.

However, the bride forever reserves her right to veto. Most grooms are happy with this inevitable arrangement.

I learned after my fifth wedding that, as DJ, you have a hundred-word limit before people start tuning you out. You're not the show, just the facilitator. When you make an announcement, you don't ask, you tell. Whether it's an announcement about remembering to sign the guest book or that the bride and groom will soon be cutting the cake, you must always be sincere and direct. You must establish yourself as a necessary agent for the reception to reach fruition. Take pride! You're representing, by extension, the entire wedding party and family, be they rich or poor, black or white, gay or straight, or any mixture thereof. If you can lock down these simple concepts you can be spinning discs and making money tomorrow.

Also, keep in mind that, while an individual person can be smart, a group of people are not. Guests at receptions are like preschoolers or a herd of sheep, take your pick. You encourage them with simple, one-step directions. You praise them for complying and reinforce their good behavior with rewards, like opening the buffet or directing them to the open bar. Your job is to be the border collie and keep the masses moving in the right direction.

My experience? If you can clearly explain to any group of people where the booze, the food, and the bathroom are, they'll follow you until the final song of the evening, or maybe even to the White House. Nobody leaves early when I DJ a wedding.

The couple eventually entered the old steelworks forty-five minutes late. Introductions were made, and the reception was primed and ready. The arsonists disguised as catering staff began lighting the candles on the tables. I anticipated the implosion and fiery death of all inside. At least the stout metal doors would keep the inferno from spreading outside our tinderbox. We'd perish, but at least the cherished and subsidized artist lofts downtown would be safe.

The buffet opened, people laughed, beer flowed, and oh how they danced. This was going to be an easy one, I thought. Even the nagging of the maid of honor was tolerable; she was in the habit of reminding me every twenty minutes that the bride really, really liked Prince. They were a great crowd. Fun.

After most guests had eaten I made my way over to the buffet table and helped myself to some chicken breast, rice pilaf, and Caesar salad. Due to overcooking, the couple's late arrival, or simply bad preparation, the food wasn't so good. The rice was bland, the salad wilted, the chicken dry. But it was free.

Later I was asked to read a statement of inspiration and gratitude from the couple to their family and guests. While waiting for my cue I took my last bite of rice pilaf and the world's driest chicken. Then I was given the signal to begin from the Prince-loving maid of honor. I took a quick sip of wine to clear my throat.

While I was still chewing some of the fossilized chicken, I started the announcement. I felt what may have been a small bone and pushed it into my cheek. I got the crowd quiet, and after complimenting the couple, the parents, and guests for coming, I proceeded to read aloud the inspirational statement.

It was a love letter. A heartfelt expression from the bride to her groom and both of their families. It was very personal and highly sentimental. When I got to the part in the message where the bride was describing how her stepmother had pulled her up from a living hell, out of the shitholes of depression, like a cigarette burning during an eclipse, had helped light her way out of the darkest caves of addiction, the piece of chicken slowly began sliding down my throat. I was reading the bride's quote of affirmation "Where there's hope, you will always find love," when the chicken decided to nest on my trachea.

I began to choke. The 250 guests thought I was choked up. But I was dying. A collective "ahh" swept across the venue as the panic in my disco began to rise. I couldn't breathe, and my eyes began to water. I tried to speak—nothing. A second chorus of "ahhh" resounded through the metal works. The bride and groom believed I was unable to continue, due to emotional incapacitation. They raced over and began hugging me. They were so touched.

I've always feared death. The Lutheran church I attended as a youth had left a lot of the end-of-life stuff rather vague. What if Jehovah had had a witness or the book of Mormon was more than just a musical?

As consciousness was beginning to fade, my eternal soul began seeing light at the end of the wedding venue. Through the mist, I could see a growing glimmer where the old widow-maker had been. The clapping grew louder. The guests were encouraging me to take the walk into the light. An apparition stood in the portal, beckoning to me with a welding torch. I remembered the blood-stain that had once been the metalworker.

A burp of wine-vomit mixed with rice pilaf and spiced with Caesar dressing brought me back to semiconsciousness. I swallowed, and the chicken went down for good. I went on to finish the letter, only now in the broken voice of asphyxiation. As I read, tears from my near-death experience rained down like rice thrown at a wedding. After reading the final verse of the soliloquy, both extended families ran out for an enthusiastic group embrace. So much love. All the guests applauded graciously, not a dry eye in the house. I was just glad to be alive. The rest of the reception was heavenly.

The wedding couple invited me to spend Christmas with their extended family for the next several years. We'd grown so close over such a short period of time. I declined, however, to attend the birth of their third child. Two was plenty. The metalworks burned to the ground (due to arson) a year after the wedding and was rebuilt as a condominium. As for me, two of the unmarried couples at the wedding asked me to be the DJ for their weddings the following year. As for the tip? Suffice it to say that my father could have bought a hell of a lot of flat bar.

THE WOODLAND AVENUE
CONFIDENTIAL

ON WOODLAND AVENUE the Druckers' dairy truck delivered milk in returnable glass bottles. The Watkins man strolled freely around our neighborhood selling household cleaners and sweetened syrup for children's drinks. Dad went to work, Mom fixed dinner. The many uses of Tupperware were revealed to me in our living room by our next-door neighbor. Mom sold Avon in the afternoons. Everybody went to church on Sunday, even the Mormon family up the hill. What could ever go wrong on Woodland Avenue?

In my neighborhood most of the families were just like mine—one dad, one mom, and a couple kids. Three houses down were the Gallaghers, and they had eleven children. My mom explained that the Gallaghers were Catholic, and that's what happened to you if you were a Catholic. God gave you a lot of kids. She explained that being a Lutheran gave you more choices. She never went into any details, though. Next to our house lived the only family in the whole neighborhood with a stepdad.

In the afternoons, Mom would pile my older sister, brother, and me into our old Ford to sell Avon. The '42 Ford was bought as a second car for $150 and made drivable through bailing wire and my father's sweat equity on the weekends. My family, minus Dad, would venture out in our Ford hoping to sell the latest beauty secrets.

Although only five, I already knew the ins and outs of wrinkle cream and the importance of using moisturizer. Mom said my testimonials made her top seller of the month. Sometimes we'd solicit our products to women who, as my mother put it, had bad skin and that I should try not to stare. Some of our older clients had lost their husbands. Just like our neighbor, Tommy's mom, Delorice. My brother and I even made up a little song: "De-lor-ice who had a div-or-us."

A few of these women were prone to buying a lot of creams and makeup that they never seemed to wear. Sure as anything, my mom would sell a trunkload of makeup to a lady named Loraine. Two weeks later she was asking to buy more. She must have used up all the makeup, because she'd never be wearing any when we showed up. But she'd buy more. They always did.

I think these nice ladies just needed to find another husband or maybe get a dog so they wouldn't be so lonely.

There was a Texaco gas station on the corner of Woodland Avenue and 104th Street. It was owned and operated by an older man with no front teeth. While filling up our Ford, he'd smoke cigarettes and tell me jokes I didn't understand. At thirty-three cents a gallon it took one and a half cigarettes to put in five dollars of gas.

On occasion, us kids would get a free packet of M&M's from the owner for being such good customers. The eight-cent packet of candy was so large I had to hold it in both hands.

Driving away from the station, I remember sharing the seemingly bottomless packet with my family. It wasn't long before I faded into a sugary reverie, serenaded by the smell of leaded gasoline. I may have only been five, but even at that age I could detect the nuanced vapors of regular and ethyl gasoline. The increase in octane and addition of lead to the ethyl was obvious. To misidentify these two types of gasoline would be like confusing a pinot with a merlot.

In the spring, 112th Street was torn up so the county could put in natural-gas lines. My mother said it was a good thing having to suffer the detours and rough roads. After the natural-gas lines went in we wouldn't have to pay those outlandish home-heating oil prices any longer. One day we were selling Avon on the bumpiest section of 112th. After hitting a large pothole, I accidentally swallowed the dime I'd been saving for a comic book. Never saw that dime again.

Mrs. Durkey had a turkey. Her turkey, Charlie, was terrifying. He was large and prone to attack anyone or anything coming into his yard. Mr. Durkey had died before I was born from a heart attack caused by too much smoking. Tommy, one of the older neighbor kids (the one with the stepdad), told me that Mr. Durkey wasn't really dead. He said Mrs. Durkey was a witch and that she'd turned Mr. Durkey into an evil turkey who liked to attack and kill little children.

We were told by our father to never cross the street to Mrs. Durkey's house unless we were with an adult. Even the milkman and the Watkins man steered clear of Charlie as best they could. On occasion, they were seen kicking at Charlie in order to make their appointed rounds.

One day we went to drop off some moisturizer for Mrs. Durkey before starting our afternoon sales calls.

Mom said if anybody needed moisturizer it was her. After pulling into Mrs. Durkey's driveway, Charlie flew straight at our '42 Ford, gobbling and beating his wings and trying to pull the hood ornament off with his beak and claws. My mother honked the horn, which scared Charlie, and he ran behind the garage. Mrs. Durkey wasn't home, so my mother just left the container of moisturizer on the back doorstep.

While Mom was coming back to the car, we could see Charlie coming around the garage for another attack. Mom ran, hoping to make it back to safety. It would be close. But Charlie was gaining ground.

My brother and I had both wanted BB guns for Christmas, but Mom said we were too young. I bet she wished we had a couple then! Instead, we threw handfuls of M&M's at Charlie's head. We hit him a few times and slowed him down enough so Mom was able to get back inside the car. Charlie spotted the candy and was now more interested in eating than terrorizing the neighborhood.

Backing out of the driveway, my brother and I raised our fists and yelled out the window, calling Charlie a big meanie. At dinner, Dad made us promise to never again visit Mrs. Durkey's house, even with an adult. That night I prayed that Mrs. Durkey's skin would get blistered and scaly without any more of Mom's moisturizer. She'd turn into a wicked old witch and die. Of course, the neighborhood would have to burn her.

On the Fourth of July, Woodland Avenue was set ablaze. To celebrate our nation's birthday, my family was going to barbecue hamburgers and hot dogs on our grill in the backyard. Us kids got to help make the potato and fruit salads. Dad had the day off. It was the best day of my five-year-old life when Mom surprised us all by bringing out two kinds of potato chips. Each of us even got our own can of root beer. My brother and I would get to light and hold our own sparklers when it got dark.

It was a sunny Fourth of July, which meant it wouldn't get dark until later in the evening. I was sitting in the front yard with my brother burning ants with a magnifying glass, when Alex and Keith, from Fruitland Avenue, roared down on dirt bikes. They were in junior high and smoking cigarettes. They were in the same grade as Debbie, our first babysitter. Both boys smiled when I mentioned her name. They said Debbie was a lot of fun, then laughed. We all did.

The older boys gave all the younger kids rides up and down Woodland Avenue. When it was my turn, I got to climb on the back of the faster bike driven by Alex. He had a bitchin' 100cc YZ Yamaha. Alex could also drive and smoke at the same time. Cool. After about an hour the bikes ran out of gas, so we all just sat beside our ditch watching the boys smoke. Keith started talking about M-80s and bottle rockets. Wanting to fit in, I told them we had sparklers. Soon the boys ran out of cigarettes and decided to borrow some gas from the can in our garage. Keith and Alex were going to Debbie's house.

It was early evening by the time the boys rode off, and there wasn't enough sun left to burn any ants. So I decided to try burning ants with a sparkler. My parents were in the house watching the evening news about Vietnam and the Kennedys, so it was easy to sneak into the garage and grab a couple sparklers. They were located right next to the propane tanks and gasoline.

It took forever for the sparkler to light, but when it did it was magical. Burning ants was much easier this way. The sparkler burned down and went out, so we lit another one. This one burned with a red color and got really hot. So we threw it into the ditch. The flames jumped up, burning all the dry grass. The sparkler must have landed on the same spot where the boys had been pouring gasoline into their dirt bikes.

My brother and I began to panic, as the fire moved toward our house and down the ditch to our grass field. I remember my dad warning that if the field caught fire in the heat of summer, the whole neighborhood would burn like hell. Mrs. Durkey was out giving Charlie some water and lumbered over with her garden hose to try putting out the fire. Mr. Thornbird, who lived next to Mrs. Durkey, went to turn on his lawn sprinkler.

Finally, Dad looked out the window, between scenes of Vietnam War footage, and saw his own yard ablaze. He ran outside and grabbed our picnic blanket and started swatting the fire, hoping to smother the flames. The Schmidts jumped out of their above-ground pool yelling "fire!" The Gallaghers showed up with all eleven kids, even the toddler, and formed a bucket brigade, throwing water on the blaze dipped from the Schmidts' swimming pool. Due to the efforts of our protestant neighbors and the Gallaghers we saved the field and the neighborhood from burning. Our ditch, though, was scorched to hell.

Dad and the other adults wanted to know what had happened. And then they started to investigate. My brother and I kept our mouths shut. Luckily for us, nobody noticed the sparkler wires or burned matches. But Mr. Thornbird found a couple smoldering cigarette butts, just as Alex and Keith came roaring down the road, Debbie riding behind Alex smoking a cigarette.

Well, hell hath no fury like a white middle-class neighborhood with a burned ditch. All the adults lit into the teenagers. It was obvious to those over thirty that the fire had been started due to the evils of teenage smoking. Furthermore, these hippies from Fruitland Avenue were probably the cause of all the problems on Woodland Avenue. Tommy having a stepdad, the Thornbirds' crabgrass, the Schmidts' pool water turning yellow, and, of course, the theft of the baby Jesus from the Gallagher's nativity scene last December.

Mrs. Durkey was the first to turn her hose on those damn Fruitland Avenue kids. Both Mr. and Mrs. Thornbird began throwing clumps of crabgrass. The Schmidts just continued to yell, while the Gallaghers formed a bucket brigade and began dousing the delinquents with the Schmidts' yellow pool water. "Go back to Fruitland Avenue!" we all screamed. And sure enough, after the hippies held up their middle fingers, they roared off down the street and were gone for good.

After it got dark, Dad made us light our sparklers in the gravel driveway, his new garden hose nearby.

A week later the entirety of Woodland Avenue was torn up. The county was putting in new water pipes as the old were said to contain too much lead. The county water crew was made up of six large men in hardhats. They smoked a lot and taught all the neighbor kids some new ways to swear. They had all kinds of neat equipment, like bulldozers and backhoes. While they were working on the street in front of our yard, I pretended to dig and lay my own water pipe using my Tonka trucks. I don't think Dad ever found his new water hose.

One morning the crew was digging in front of Mrs. Durkey's house and met Charlie. At first, they just ignored him. But after the man who smoked and swore the most, probably the foreman, got attacked by Charlie, we heard more swearing than usual, followed by a loud gobbling noise, then a lot of smoking and an early lunch. I didn't see or hear Charlie for the rest of the day. At dinner, my mom said that Charlie had gone away to live on a turkey farm far, far away. We could now trick-or-treat at Mrs. Durkey's house again. Hooray!

Later that evening, while experiencing abdominal pain and constipation from drinking tap water, Tommy came over. Between my frequent trips to the bathroom, Tommy told me what had really happened to Charlie. The crew digging up our road were really special army guys who had been fighting in Vietnam. While there, they'd killed thousands of Viet Cong. As I wasn't allowed to watch the evening news, I had to ask Tommy what a Viet Cong was. He told me the Vietcong were communists who looked a lot like King Kong, only smaller. They lived in Quebec, Canada, where the war was being fought. So the tough guys on the work crew were really Vietnam veterans. Wow!. In the war they'd worn green berets, just like my sister, and had killed a lot of Viet Kongs. I figured they had to smoke and swear so much in order to feel normal like the rest of us. Wow!

On that fateful day, Tommy said Charlie attacked the work crew and was grabbed by his neck before he could peck anyone. Charlie was thrown to the ground, then got his head bashed in with a shovel. They buried Charlie half-alive, along with the new water pipe and some cig-arette butts. Tommy said that if you stood in front of Mrs. Durkey's house you could still hear the faint gob-bling. And, if you dared to stand on the same spot at midnight on Halloween and spoke Charlie's name three times, the hand of Mr. Durkey would come rising up to drag you down to hell.

In August, my mother began working part-time at JCPenney. So my brother, sister, and me were babysat by another junior-high girl from Fruitland Avenue named Suzy. During the second week a lot went wrong. We awoke one morning to find a dead man lying in our front yard flat on his back wearing shabby clothes. At first, I thought someone had dug up old Mr. Durkey. Or worse, that a half-dead Charlie had dug himself out of the ground, only to transform back into Mr. Durkey, who then died again after smoking too many cigarettes.

We all thought he was dead. My brother said if you yelled really loud you could wake the dead. As loud as we could, we began yelling that it was time to rise and shine, hoping to wake him. He didn't move.

Tommy came over and said he'd poked the body with a stick and that the dead man wasn't breathing. Suzy was convinced that the man had been hit by a car. My brother and sister were sure he'd suffered a heart attack due to lifestyle choices and too much smoking. But I knew the truth. It was death by Bigfoot.

The man had probably been making out with some lady in a 1965 GT Mustang Fastback, before being besieged by a herd of Bigfoots. The hapless couple then tried to escape in their Mustang with a 271-horsepower engine and four-speed racing transmission. But the Bigfoots caught them. They always did. Then came the bashing part. After first bashing the lady's head through the windshield, they tried to catch the man, but he managed to escape on foot. He probably died from exhaustion. The Bigfoots were probably planning to steal a 1965 Mustang GT sometime later and drive back to bash the dead man's head through the windshield.

Suzy called the police station, while Tommy went off to find a bigger stick. Ten minutes later the county sheriff showed up. He managed to wake the man by poking him with his nightstick. After placing the man in the patrol car, the officer came over and told us what was really going on. He explained that the man was homeless and had passed out after leaving a tavern on Fruitland Avenue earlier that morning. We were relieved to hear that the man was alive and that he'd be taken to get a warm meal and have a place to sleep. Soon Woodland Avenue was back to normal. Tommy showed up a minute too late dragging an eight-foot two-by-four stolen from the Gallagher's garage.

After the police officer left, Tommy told me what had really happened. He said it wasn't Bigfoots at all but that it was the Manson Family. He informed me that Charles Manson had been seen in the neighborhood after escaping from prison. Charles and his family were trying to persuade small children, like myself, to smoke the devil's lettuce (marijuana). This, we all knew, led to harder drugs.

After a child succumbed to Mr. Manson's reefer madness, they'd be strapped to the saddle of addiction like Judy Garland. Charles would then lead his strung-out army of elementary-school misfits through the poppy fields of Oz. Once there, you'd be forced to worship the devil. Then you'd begin chasing down 1965 Mustangs and bashing the hapless victims' heads through the windshields over and over like a homicidal Bigfoot. After that, he said, the military would send you to Vietnam.

That September, I started half days of kindergarten. While waiting for the bus on the first day of school, I ran into the neighborhood bully, Dean Kemper. He was in the third grade and always mad about everything. If the bus was late, he got mad. If the bus was early, he got mad. If you said hello or stood in the wrong spot at the bus stop, he got mad. So on the third day of school, I told Dean the badly needed truth—that he had a mighty bad temper. That was also the day he threw me into the Woodland Avenue ditch.

I ran home crying. After cleaning me up, my mom drove me to school in the '42 Ford and let the principal have it. My mother wasn't paying taxes so that a thug from Fruitland Avenue could bully and nearly drown her youngest son. Dean was called out of Mr. Carson's third-grade classroom and made to apologize. Mr. Gallagher, the principal, threatened to give Dean a swat if he did it again. As punishment, Dean was forced to stand by himself at the bus stop in a designated area next to the fire hydrant for a whole month.

It wasn't long before things got back to normal on Woodland Avenue. During the second week of kindergarten, I got the chance to participate in my first duck-and-cover drill. Tommy said my school was fourteen miles away from a major air force base as the nuclear missile flies. My entire class thought it was exhilarating to spontaneously hide beneath our desks, folding ourselves into little balls. Mrs. Harris, my kindergarten teacher, would wipe a tear from her eye every time she came out from under her desk.

The Druckers' dairy truck continued to pick up our empty milk bottles. The Watkins man was no longer walking and drove a Chevrolet from house to house. Fewer moms were staying home. Dad went to work, and my mother became employed full time at JCPenney as a bookkeeper. She still fixed dinner. Almost everybody went to church on Sunday, even the Mormon family up the hill. What could ever go wrong on Woodland Avenue?

ON THE THIRD DAY
HE RESTED

T HE WIFE REMINDED me for the 99th time that the band gear had to go. "All of it," she said into the basement. I don't really know the mathematical or theoretical significance of the number 99 except that it is one less than a century, which is how long it felt that I had been having this discussion with my wife. Ba da boom.

I looked at the audio disarray around me and fantasized over what God must have felt like looking down on his creation on, say, the third day. The earth not yet completed, perhaps still bundled in bins, the lord of all creation puzzling over what was good and what was evil, and whether to just throw the whole damn thing out and start over.

All that lay before me was my creation. I had purchased it, puzzled it together, and nurtured it in the corner of the garage next to the freezer and canned goods. It was part of my past, but my future? Like a true standup god, I would accept responsibility for the lingering remains of what had once been our band's humanity, if not humility.

It's not fair of you to write about the band without getting their take on things.

The band had broken up. The "we" of the band's relationship had become a lonely "I" leaving me to deal with the sound equipment as I saw fit. Yes, I owned all of the equipment, but they, the band, the others, had allowed us to generate musical greatness, for a time. We had been a glam heavy metal band and rocked the west coast for over ten years. We did mostly covers, a few originals, and recorded a few CDs that received minor airplay. Anyone remember "Crimson Angel"? We were also infamous for the band having the biggest and best hair.

I was the bass player: the bottom of the band, the anchor, the ramrod, both the rock and the roll. I cofounded the band with Mathias the guitar player and Walt the vocalist in 1980. Over the decades we cycled through five different drummers. Our last drummer was Zeke.

Zeke and I played well together. He had great hair. We grooved and kept good time for most of the songs we played. But after Zeke joined the band, I became aware of the difference between keeping good time and being on time. He was always late to our gigs. Always. On several occasions Zeke would back his van up to the stage door mere moments before we were set to play.

Zeke got more attention from the ladies than you did. Is that what this is about?

The public address system, or "PA" as it is referred to by those in the business, gave voice and life to the band. It consisted of the main speakers, the stage monitors, and a vanload of amplifiers, microphones, mic stands, and guitar stands. We had procured over the years an enormous quantity of guitar and microphone cords that would allow us to play from our garage rehearsal space into another county should we have wished to do so. Yes, we had lots of cords. Soon after starting the band I also became the sound guy.

My bandmates treated PAs like crap. At the end of the night they would often throw speakers and equipment into the van like they were loading firewood. We were replacing a speaker or power amp every fifth gig or so due to misuse.

Eventually I got tired of spending my Saturdays soldering and duct taping speakers and just bought the whole damned PA. I became the sole owner of all the equipment. I negotiated an extra fifteen percent of the total gig money since I was providing and setting up the PA. I figured I could get paid twice for each gig and have more free time on the weekends.

You were being greedy.

As any sound engineer can tell you, a great PA can make the crappiest band sound good or a mediocre band, like ours, sound like pros. Our progress through the metal scene was due, in large part, to my attention to the selection of equipment and detailed setup and placement of the speakers. If anyone was going to blow the speakers or overheat the amps it was going to be me.

I mixed the band's sound from the stage on the fly, relying on a single monitor playing the house mix. For the bigger shows, we had to hire out and split the cost with the other bands renting the same venue.

For a typical show, I'd usually, single-handedly, be responsible for carrying, loading, driving, unloading, carrying again, and setting up three thousand pounds of sound gear for the rest of the band. The joy for me as bass player, and now sound guy, was that at the end of the night while my bandmates were getting free beers and flirting with coquettish women dressed in lingerie and leather skirts, I got to do the whole thing over again, only in reverse. Break down, carry, load, drive, unload, carry... you get the idea.

I realize I was being paid twice, but these musical purists wouldn't even raise a drumstick to help. Mathias, our guitarist, would experience artistic throes that would necessitate having to put on new strings, followed by precision tuning, which could go on for days.

Our lead singer, Walt, would often experience constrictions in his vocals cords; he was convinced this was the beginning of throat cancer. Walt would take preventative therapy by gargling and sucking on the hard candies I brought to our gigs. Apparently, it's impossible to enjoy a sugary confection and help unload equipment or even attach one's own microphone to the cord I conveniently laid out for him.

Walt was diabetic, and you gave him candy?

Often, I'd look up to discover that no one from the band was anywhere to be found. They were prone to disappearing, for as long as forty minutes, to spontaneously urinate as a collective prior to a performance.

Chronic urination is a sign of diabetes.

One of my more agonizing vocations as sound guy was that I also had to critique the sound quality of my bandmates. After all the equipment had been set up, the vocalist and the lead guitar player would be manically concerned with their sound quality, their mic, and their amplifier arrangements.

Both Walt and Mathias had major hearing damage.

Upon receiving any request regarding sound critiquing, I'd usually stare vacantly as if I'd not heard the question, then nod. After a time, they grew to understand that this meant their sound was good. I'd adjust the sound of the band at the mixing board anyway, and it would sound fantastic. It always did.

You always had a great ear. You were a very good bass player and sound tech.

I was a lonely, somewhat bitter man toward the end of our relationship.

You were all self-centered assholes!

"We," the band, had broken up again because of our mammoth egos. And because anomalies involving wives, girlfriends, family, and career had reached critical mass.

Most guys joined a band to play music, party, and meet women, not necessarily in that order. But in the case of the ladies, after you meet them, you may begin dating them, living with them, and, on rare occasion, marrying them. So, the very reason you joined a band often becomes the reason the band breaks up. Or, at the very least, changes the lineup.

John Lennon stated in an interview that he didn't give the Beatles five years before they'd inevitably split. They lasted ten. Quite the accomplishment, but keep in mind that Yoko showed up around year seven or eight.

I'd check the historical accuracy of this claim. Many rock historians believe they met much earlier, in 1966.

Children are even more toxic to a band than women. If you don't have children but are pondering the idea, stop reading now. Having children slowly kills your artistic dreams. We all start out thinking we can balance the day job with the band and a family, but we can't.

In 1980, you could perform on a Friday and Saturday night, hire a good sound guy, get your hair properly teased for the show, drink some beer, and still have a Franklin or two in everybody's wallet come Sunday. By the mid-'80s the money available for live music was already drying up. By 1995, most bands, regardless of genre, could barely break even after a three-day weekend of shows. Most bands had CDs or cassettes to sell at the performances to keep finances in the black.

Even a mediocre or lousy band could play for a modest amount and sell enough merchandise to keep the band on the road. The dream of making it big was being replaced with the reality of making ends meet. The hard rock and metal crowds were getting older. The younger fans were nostalgic but piercing tin ears.

Sad, but true.

The same equipment that had been making my band sound better was now becoming more affordable, lighter, and portable. Venues no longer wanted to bring in a stage or even a single riser. Smaller venues without a stage could hire a portable DJ and have music any night of the week without having to move the pool tables or the *Pac-Man* machine. Also, club owners using a DJ could now dial in a different genre every night of the week. Country on Wednesday, queer disco on Thursday, rock or metal on Friday, and hip-hop on Saturday. A DJ could rock the house for a third of the money. People drank while dancing to DJ grooves the same as they did to a band.

Most of the live music scene that I'd known throughout the '80s and early '90s was sadly being replaced by nonpaying gigs. By 2000, most live music experiences were reduced to a single performer singing while playing their acoustic guitar at an open mic on Monday evenings.

Professional musicians busking on the street was just around the corner.

Most garage bands are perpetually getting started or in the process of breaking up. Though there is a midpoint, albeit usually a short one, when there is complete balance, an equilibrium of purpose and direction.

It's a small window of time when the music sounds and feels great regardless of whether you have a Yoko or not. Sadly, our window had closed.

I think you really should double-check the Yoko Ono timeline.

I stood in the garage looking at my life through a lens of electronics. What to do? There was no longer a "them" or an "us" or a "we." But there was still a "me" and a whole lot of sound equipment.

You could always become a DJ.

"Are you speaking to me now or at me?"

Yes.

"Why a DJ?"

Let the speakers be your voice, the amplifiers your heart and strength, and the speaker cables the very sinew for the conveyance of your electric blood.

"Who wrote that?"

If you don't start making money, your wife will make you sell the equipment.

"What about the band?"

They were all assholes, remember? You don't need the "them," the "us," or the "we."

"And then what? Play techno downtown?"

No. Don't be just any DJ. Be "The Wedding DJ."

"But I've never DJ'd."

So what? You got married not knowing what to do.

"Okay. But I hate canned music."

You'll get used to it. You're my phoenix. Now rise from the heavy-metal ashes.

"Yes."

No longer would I respond to a drummer's request for not one, but two microphones on his drum set. The diabetic, future-cancer-victim vocalist would have to bring his own damn microphone and hard candies. And as for the guitars? This stooge would no longer be there to turn them up or down. I'd turn them all off.

For a hundred bucks you'd still whore yourself out to any band that needed a PA.

Having over a decade of experience as the sound tech for the band, I quickly assembled a crude, but powerful, DJ set up. I brought the multidisc CD player we used for church service out from the living room and, four RCA plugs later, I was ready. I pressed the play button and was unceremoniously brought to Jesus by a bone-crushing version of "This Little Gospel Light of Mine," which apparently had been left in the player. The volume on the player was set to eleven. The sound was deafening. The subwoofers trembled like thunderclouds, the main speakers responding in kind like a chorus of vengeful angels screaming blasphemy at the idea of not letting that little gospel light shine, shine, shine.

My wife came into the garage and asked me what I was doing. The garage has traditionally been my place of worship, my sanctuary, my space to poke around for hours with chainsaws, lawnmowers, drill motors, and other potentially castrating tools of husbandry. The house, I discovered shortly after our marriage, was all hers.

Nice sexist stereotype.

"What are you doing?" she yelled over the popular children's hymn that hinted at the possibility of salvation, or arson. Maybe both.

This is a really weak allegory.

"Thinking about being a wedding DJ!" I shouted over the fading chorus.

"Great," she said, "just so long as I can park the Civic."

So, it begins?

"So it begins."

IN VINO VERITAS

T HE POET OGDEN Nash once wrote that "candy is dandy, but liquor is quicker." The meaning of the phrase is simple. One can use alcohol to influence another. In the old days, a few drinks were seen as the quickest way to win someone's heart or maybe get them into bed. Employing this tactic today, though, you might find that it's the quickest way to go to jail or meet the "Me Too" movement. To the county medical examiner, distilled spirits was the pivotal factor that encouraged Nurse Tracy to leave the road at a high rate of speed following a Christmas party. Alcohol has long been referred to as a "social lubricant."

When I hear any reference to lubrication, I immediately think about 1970s television. Being left alone as a child of seven, during the carefree summer daze, I'd watch a lot of daytime television. In the morning, there were reruns of *Bonanza* on the local station and lots of game shows on the major networks. There was *Gambit*, hosted by perpetually smiling Wink Martindale (check out that polyester) and *Wizard of Odds*, hosted by a very young Alex Trebek. There was also *The Price is Right* and *Jeopardy!* with original host Art Fleming. And who could forget the lovable but goofy celebrity guests like Soupy Sales on *$25,000 Pyramid* or *Hollywood Squares* with George

Gobel, Rose Marie, and, of course, Paul Lynde? X gets the center square.

As the networks approached high noon, the fun of pretending to be a cowboy and hanging out with Little Joe and Lorne Greene on *Bonanza* came to an end, like all childish things. The good-natured sport and spirit of game shows like *Match Game, Shoot for the Stars*, and *Let's Make a Deal* faded to human drama and the tragedy of afternoon television.

They were called soap operas, and even at seven, I knew they were dirty. It was like watching a Lysol or Ty-D-Bol commercial. The toilet seat seemed clean, but after looking much closer through the magical magnifying lens of 1970s special effects, you could see the filth. Yep, all the Tide in Mom's laundry room couldn't soak or scour out the immoral stain and depravity of afternoon programming. Maybe if Madge, that huckster for Palmolive dishwashing liquid, combined forces with Shout, Ty-D-Bol, Scrubbing Bubbles, and Mom, they might together reduce the immoral blight of the afternoon soaps. They could clean up the smut while gently preparing one's hands for a manicure. As for salacious afternoon television? We were soaking in it.

The plots, so loosely called, were easy enough to follow, but the storytelling was just too segmented and slow. So, at age seven, I decided to create my own soap opera: *The Days of Our Doctors Living on the Edge from Another World at Night as the World Turned with One Life to Live at General Hospital Star Trek.*

Season one: Janice, a blonde pretending to be eighteen (who was really sixteen) lies about her age in order to strip at a club called Passions located downtown in Shady Valley.

Director's note: Janice should be portrayed by a busty actress in her twenties.

Janice, an underage stripper, falls in love with Jim, formerly a man of the cloth she meets at Passions. Jim's reluctantly attending a bachelor party at the strip club for Leonard. Backstory. Jim had saved Leonard from committing suicide months before. Leonard is slowly pulling his life together after battling a heroin addiction, womanizing, and overcoming flashbacks caused by his two tours in Vietnam. Leonard eventually meets his future wife, the upstanding and recently widowed Nyota, also working at the inner-city outreach center. Leonard is hoping to give something back by helping the inner-city people in need. Leonard is street-smart and used to watch *Soul Train*, which impressed Nyota. He's able to get down and jive with just about anybody. He drops words like "groovy" and phrases like "outta sight" and "I'm down with that." Far out!

While Janice is working the pole at Passions for Leonard's bachelor party, Jim looks up to see the fallen angel—Janice. As the music plays, Jim and Janice catch each other's eye. It will be love at first pole dance.

Director's note: Five-minute cut-to-the-left, cut-to-the-right camera war with both actors winking and smiling blindingly white, perfect teeth. Camera zooms in on both for split-screen close-ups, faces softened with filters.

As the sensuous stripping song continues, Janice now dances only for Jim. After they finish, Janice wants to change, and Jim walks outside to smoke a cigarette. Thus begins the struggle with his pea-sized conscience. Should he save Janice from stripping and face temptations of the flesh or return to the priesthood and renew his pledge of celibacy? He will share his personal agony with the audience over three episodes, pretending to speak to God. He will eventually and regretfully choose Janice.

Director's note: Have Jim break the fourth wall looking directly into the camera. Unfiltered camera - eyes tearful and bloodshot.

Actor's note: Have Jim insert unnecessary pauses while speaking, often emphasizing, words, of, no, particular, importance, for, no, particular, reason.

Things heat up in episode four. Unbeknownst to Jim, Janice really wants to have coitus. Whenever she tries to seduce him, Jim replies that he can't because of how much he honors her as a child of God. In episode five, Jim faces his greatest temptation as Janice drops her bathrobe, giving Jim and the afternoon fan base some much-needed gratuitous nudity. She offers. He honors. She offers. He honors. Off her and on her, off her and on her, all episode long. Fade to black. Both actors are absent from the show for three episodes to build suspense.

On the other side of Shady Valley, Spock's losing Christine. Wanting to live life yet again to the fullest, Christine begins dating Spock following their whirlwind weekend of wild coitus in Monte Carlo. After returning to Shady Valley with Spock, Christine agrees to be his Delta Dawn and live with him in his mansion in the sky. There, she enjoys a life of riches, afternoon coitus, and privilege previously unknown to her. Her feelings for Spock are logical and at times ambivalent. But her desire to continue the lifestyle of the rich and famous is love at first cocktail party.

Over the last several years Christine has scribbled down memoirs containing intimate feelings and broken dreams regarding her tragic first marriage to Scotty, the desperate affirmations of a woman trying to find meaning in life after so much loss. Scotty, unbeknownst to Christine, has been working for the FBI, not working side by side with Leonard helping the inner-city brothers and sisters. He's mortally wounded in a drug bust, shot by a dealer who'd been selling heroin to Leonard, not killed in a tragic car accident. Having prior training as a nurse, Christine was immediately suspicious. She insists on visiting the coroner's office to examine the body. Upon her arrival, it's revealed that someone had stolen Scotty's corpse. Is this an attempt to cover up his secret FBI affiliation? If so, by whom?

During a gala celebrating Spock's 140th birthday, Sulu, the regal, handsome, down-on-his-luck, British novelist playboy slips away from the party and ransacks Spock and Christine's bedroom. While looking for roofies, painkillers, and quaaludes, Sulu accidentally discovers Christine's memoirs. He begins reading the magical prose of redemption and manages to stop, at least momentarily, his obsession with drugs. Sulu consummately falls in love with Christine. She had his adoration at "Dear Diary."

Jim and Janice, now a couple, go out dancing at the club called Powder.

Director's note: For the Powder scene, just hang a different sign in the background. Rearrange the same chairs and tables used at Passions. Use the same extras, but have them switch clothes.

Jim has given up the priesthood for good, while Janice

drinks gin and tonics, much to the distaste of the former. Jim will later, in episode ten, be reduced to shooting heroin himself in order to handle his carnal guilt from having twice-daily coitus with Janice, along with his own personal demons from his tours in Vietnam. At Powder, a song familiar to Janice begins to play. Her old life as a stripper comes flooding back to her in an emotional deluge. Tipsy, Janice feels the need to strip once more. Jim's unable to stop her. The mostly male crowd begins catcalling and cheering, telling her to dance. That would be all the encouragement Janice would need. Slowly, she begins to untie the knot of her sexy halter dress.

Meanwhile, Christine shares a drink with Sulu at a corner table, away from prying eyes and disapproving glances. The now-alcoholic Christine also hears Janice's stripping song, which coincidentally was also the song she and Spock first experienced coitus to during that magical weekend in Monte Carlo. Racked by guilt, she accepts the two quaaludes offered to her by Sulu, chasing both pills with her gin and tonic.

Sulu stages an unsuccessful overdose for Christine in an attempt to steal her now-promising novel and revive his sagging literary career. The next morning Christine wakes up naked in bed with Sulu, not remembering whether or not she had coitus. And what of her newly-wed husband, Spock?

I was forced to go back to elementary school to attend the second grade, thus ending season one. But as foreshadowed earlier in the season, the DJ playing the life-crushing song at Powder would be the very same one who had been spinning discs at Passions. Also, this same morally devoid entertainer had been selling heroin to

Leonard, prior to pulling the trigger on Scotty. We all know moral corruption always begins with a DJ.

The combination of alcohol and music is always an interesting mix, often unpredictable. The social lubricant for a great wedding reception on Friday may lead to fisticuffs on Saturday, recycling the same playlist. People who drink often drink best. If a twenty-five-year-old is used to downing three cold ones several times a week, I'm not worried about him tipping six during the reception. These guests are what I call my "good drinkers." Once the music starts they'll dance to anything with no complaints.

Unfortunately, for every happy drinker there's their counterpart. The yin to the yang. Remember Rip Van Winkle, that henpecked bastard and beleaguered drunk? Rip runs into the woods with his dog. Is he hunting squirrels or considering a darker way out of his marriage? Accidental shooting? To shoot, perchance to dream? But before he can take his plan to fruition, he meets some hobbits carrying a rum keg and goes off to party with Bilbo and some of the dwarf guys. A few drinks later, he meets the rest of the cast from *The Lord of the Rings*.

Question. Did the absence of female characters in the hobbit movies concern anyone but me? Lifestyle choices aside, Mr. Peter Jackson, how can you keep killing thousands of Middle-earth's finest in every movie without addressing the supply side?

I don't want to see the actual mating of hobbits or dwarfs. That would be perverted and weird. Just show a little more family time and home life. How about Maury pushing Pippin on the swing while the children of Aragorn and Arwen run around the backyard playing

Kick the Orc and Hide the Precious? Then Gimli would show up with his wife and dwarf kids for some diversity. All the while the anemic Gandalf would be barbecuing like a madman.

To be honest, I would definitely buy a ticket to see a couple elves get it on, though. Maybe some mood lighting on a reconstructed set of *Rivendell.* I would envision perfumed flower petals falling from a leafy canopy encouraging the impassioned lovers into a writhing coitus. A couple close-ups of their perfectly shaped elf ears and velvety buttocks would be nice. Then maybe cut to some elf, on half-elf action in one of the waterfalls. I'd stream that.

Anyway, Rip goes on to dance the night away at what was probably a queer disco party, (that would be a plot twist for Washington Irving), has one too many rum and cokes, and wakes up after twenty years with one hell of a hangover. The happy-go-lucky hobbits just leave Rip passed out against a tree and go back to the Shire to smoke some pipe weed while waiting to film the next movie. Lesson learned? We all need access to no-fault divorce.

They say alcohol is alcohol. But I can tell you from experience that there's a clear difference between groups drinking wine and beer and those drinking the hard stuff, particularly whiskey. Before becoming a DJ, I was a musician in several bar bands and played to more than my share of intoxicated patrons. People fighting while drinking is nothing new to me. I've played every style of music from country to rock to disco. But the playlist has nothing to do with the evening's outcome or the probability of a fight. One truism I'll stick to is this: wherever you have whiskey and women in close proximity, there will be a fight. Usually, it's the men fighting over a lady. But I've seen and done it all. I witnessed two biker chicks throw punches after whiskey shots that could have gotten them on the card for the UFC. Also, this is when you tend to see weapons come out. Nobody pulls a knife after drinking a carafe of pinot noir.

In general, beer drinkers have to pee so often that it forces them to be a little nicer, drunk or not. Nobody wants to start trouble with a full bladder. Beer people, when they're drunk, just seem to get a little grabby, not so much violent.

The worst bar fight I ever saw started with a grabby beer guy getting too friendly with a pinot-drinking girl whose boyfriend was drinking whiskey. The beer guy didn't have a chance. However, his friend, who'd been taking tequila shots, chose to intervene and protect his beer buddy. Mr. Tequila and Dr. Whiskey went at it, evenly matched. Both were extremely wasted and half the time were swinging at people who just weren't there.

I once dropped off a karaoke station for a bachelorette party in a ritzy neighborhood downtown. Large house, twenty or so attendees, all women. The party broke up early due to the maid of honor fighting with the groom's sister. The sister called *me*, then the police. I entered the house just in time to keep two bridesmaids from throwing the karaoke machine out the third-floor window into the swimming pool. A quick glance at the cluttered kitchen sink and the overflowing trash bin told me all I needed to know.

Once the red zinfandel had run out and the male stripper had left, the "ladies" moved on to vodka lemon drops. After those were gone the whiskey came out. Thirty minutes later the maid of honor was kicking the crap out of the groom's sister for calling her a bitch. I DJ'd the wedding a week later. The battered bridesmaid tried to use concealer, but you could still see her blackened eye.

As a DJ my tactic for dealing with drunks is to simply turn the whole game around. I say to the person giving me grief something like, "I already played your song, what else do you want me to play?" This stops most of the extremely inebriated cold. I've asked them to make a choice for a question they never asked. The higher brain tries to kick in, but the rational thinking just isn't there. If they come back, I say, "Okay, what song do you want to hear now?" This puts most troublemakers on their heels. They basically forget why they're talking to me to begin with and decide it's just too much brain work for 1:30 in the morning. They go off in search of easier prey, like the catering staff.

If someone's really going to be a problem, I stop the music. This gets everybody's attention, especially if dancing's going on. The reception guests have been hearing something for the last three hours, now they hear nothing. That's the power of silence. Within seconds, I'm rescued. Usually a group of dancers comes over first. Occasionally, the mother of the bride rushes over to save the day. Nobody messes with her. Most people think she's nuts.

One memorable wedding was twenty miles out on Five Mile Road. A family estate on twenty-five acres butting up against a small river. The wedding was country themed. The bridal party was dressed in formal attire complimented by the accoutrements of cowboy hats and boots. After setting up, I began playing a varied selection of background music and some of the couple's requests.

Then I met Brad. Everybody met Brad. Brad was an asshole. Brad had been the one flipping shit to the photographer and the catering staff. Actually, to call this guy an asshole would be an insult to our rectums. One's asshole at least serves a purpose. Brad's only purpose was to be Brad—obnoxious.

During the ceremony Brad couldn't shut up. He talked over the pastor. He talked over the bridesmaids reading poems. He talked over the groomsmen reading scripture. His older brother, the groom, finally told him to shut the hell up in the middle of the couple exchanging vows. The bridal party and guests applauded. Brad was quiet for the rest of the ceremony. To end the rural ceremony, the country couple donned their cowboy hats and said "I do" with a do-si-do.

At the reception, Brad was everywhere. He caught the garter. He caught the bouquet. He even managed a first dance with the bride before being peeled off by the groom. His toast to the couple was so long and meandering that the batteries gave out in my cordless microphone due to boredom. But soon we were on to the dancing, and oh how they danced. Brad danced with everyone and anyone—between keg stands, that is. As I suspected, drinking beer made him a little grabby toward a few of the bridesmaids. Luckily for Brad, their partners weren't drinking whiskey or tequila. Otherwise, the night might have ended very differently.

It was near midnight. The level of drinking at this wedding had thus far been extensive. I'd been alternating AC/DC and Hank Williams Jr. for the last half hour. I was killing it. The common appeal of both artists only becomes obvious after your sixth beer. God, could these people party. During "Thunderstruck" I heard the first shot. The gun's muzzle flashed like a bolt of lightning. The report of the pistol resounded like a canon. Someone was shooting a handgun. It was Brad.

For the last hour the reception had been a celebration, no Brad. Now Brad was back in black, standing there holding a .45-caliber pistol, a flashlight under his chin, and a cup of beer in his other hand. The second and third shots caught everyone's attention. The groom ran over and quickly disarmed his brother.

Brad staggered back to the reception having lost nothing of his obnoxiousness. I think I liked him better all alone in the dark with a gun. Upon returning to the reception, Brad would surely be Brad again.

The groom had a moment of clarity. He ran from the crowd to the top of the grassy knoll behind me. He yelled "stage dive" and proceeded to run down the hill as fast as his tuxedo would allow. Using my subwoofer as a ramp, he catapulted himself into the air, soaring like an eagle. The crowd reacted quickly by moving over to catch the flying groom. He was embraced by all in a drunken revelry and slowly brought to the ground. Before anyone could burp, the bride was running down the hill, still in her wedding dress. She could fly, this angel. She landed softly, caressed by the ecstatic crowd. The happy couple fell together and passionately kissed as the guests raised their plastic cups in an elated salute to love and intoxication.

Then I heard the voice. It was Brad. He was now running down the hill toward the crowd. This drunken diva would not be denied his evening opus finale. But after Brad yelled "stage dive," the crowd parted. Brad was left soaring solo over an abyss of bad feelings and resentment. He went up, up, up, before going down, down, down. Nobody caught Brad.

Brad lay on the lawn like a blot of forgotten potato salad. He was still. He was oh, so very still. His loving brother, the groom, went over to examine the body. He turned to face the silent crowd nodding his head. Brad was gone. The groom, per country custom, appropriated a tablecloth stained with BBQ sauce to cover his brother's lifeless form. Everybody danced. Later, as Brad continued in his unconsciousness, guests began using him as a drink table placing beers on him atop coasters when dancing. The BBQ was fired up once again, and the party continued until 3:30 in the morning.

Traveling home under the morning stars, I thought about the eventful evening and 1970s game shows. I had also survived Brad. Driving to the wedding earlier in the day, I'd expected to find great BBQ and Coors Light in a picturesque country setting. But I got more, a lot more. Coming soon, the much anticipated season two of *The Days of Our Doctors Living on the Edge from Another World at Night as the World Turned with One Life to Live at General Hospital Star Trek.*

MOMMY DEAREST

W**HAT'S THE GREATEST** indicator of whether a wedding will be successful and beautiful or end up being a forty thousand-dollar fustercluck? One must look past the dollar signs and even the bride. Bridezillas do exist, and it's a bitch to work with a bitch. But if you want to measure a wedding's temperature more accurately than a rectal thermometer and predict its chance of reaching successful fruition, then look no further than the mother of the bride. Yes, these matrons of matrimony are the best indicators of what's coming your way as a DJ.

First, a Psych 202 treatise from yours truly. The information presented, I gleaned from an Abnormal Psychology class that I took following my championship year of beer pong at one of Washington's secondary colleges. Underachiever? Generation X? Got a 2.3 GPA? Fannie Mae loan? Welcome! This class exposed me to fetishes and depraved behaviors that I'd only dreamed of. It dealt with real issues, affecting real people, not just flights of my personal fancy. After finishing the course, I became an expert at diagnosing friends and classmates with a myriad of abnormal behaviors, running the gamut of personality disorders, mood disorders, pyromania, and frotteurism.

This chapter in time grew into my personal Renaissance as a fifth-year senior, which was highlighted by intricate and precise experiments involving shots of tequila, self-awareness, and improvement through conjugation with flexible coeds. Ah, higher education.

What I took away from the ninety-plus hours in Psych 202 was this: too much stress can make people weird. Even the study of abnormal behavior itself can be stressful. My own personal growth at this time was achieved through, you guessed it, stress.

My theory goes like this: abnormality exists everywhere within the sphere of humanity and in every person. Like alien embryos embedded in our chests, our propensity for perversion lies dormant until stress begins to awaken the sleeper and the mental-health monsters begin to breech our identities and psyches. Most of us are able to keep these abscesses toward the abnormal within us. But as Ridley Scott showed us in the movie *Alien*, everyone can hear you scream in space when the Xenomorph bursts out of your chest. Of course, when this happens in real life people don't infect the spaceship with alien spawn, they just get weirder. Sometimes, really weird.

So, a person's mental health is highly influenced by stress. This supposition must be wholeheartedly embraced or nothing good will come of it. Consider Dickens's Marley and Hamlet's father, both characters deemed deceased for the sake of plot and for moral purpose to prevail. Otherwise, Tiny Tim might as well have been run over by a steam engine, and our dear Hamlet may have simply eaten hallucinogenic mushrooms while slumming about the state of Denmark.

My theory continues: one's ability to handle stress, real or perceived, is not contingent on the size of one's brain but on the size of one's spring. Your spring, simply put, is your ability to "just deal with it," the "it" being whatever real or perceived thing that causes you stress. The bigger the spring the more stress you can endure. It's really the ability to push back and hold the abnormal monsters within your chest and prevent them from crushing the part that makes you, you.

But as my time working in the YMCA locker room has taught me, springs, like other things in nature, come in a variety of sizes. There are small springs, medium springs, fat and skinny springs, and, of course, the oh-my-god-where-do-you-find-a-screwdriver-for-tightening-that springs? Remember that all people have a spring and, much like other things, size matters.

If you want to see normal people crack, simply turn up the stress high enough to surpass their spring strength and watch them pop. Provide enough stress, actual or perceived, and even the toughest kernel will eventually crack. This includes our dark inner thoughts, negative emotions, and the parts of us that nobody else should ever see. Our spring helps to keep us smiling and cool-headed when dealing with rush-hour traffic, dumb bosses or, say, obnoxious relatives you only see at weddings.

I've noticed this even within my own enlightened self and consider it an unequivocal fact. Overwork me for a couple weeks, cut back my sleep, throw in a dick of a boss, nagging spouse, or a rotating schedule, and I'll assuredly become agitated, angry, and develop a propensity for delusions. Next comes the paranoia and anger. After that, well, everything gets a little fuzzy. Yes, I become a furry. So, good job, medium-size spring.

Despite the intricate planning and unsolicited help from friends, pulling off a successful wedding is one of the most stressful experiences, period. Thus the propensity for mental abnormality among those participating in the endeavor. Planning a wedding involves consensus between bride and groom, figuring out who to invite, who to exclude, and many other niceties, customs, and notions. And, of course, who's paying for the whole damn thing? As any alchemist knows, money and family don't often mix. Ultimately, everything depends on your catalyst: the couple.

This chemistry, which may provide us with a loving and beautiful pairing, followed by adorable grandchildren, can often become unstable and explosive, even dangerous. This instability is often first exhibited by the bride's mother. If Mommy Dearest is the one planning, or worse, paying for the wedding, then the stage has been set for the perfect mental-breakdown maelstrom. The forecast? Psychosis with a chance of filicide.

The wedding. Dysfunction aside, this is where the mother of the bride really shines. She's covert and svelte, a behind-the-scenes presence. She's truly in the trenches and, much like a seasoned staff sergeant, is responsible for a lot of the dirty work but fails to receive a medal or mention for battles fought. To be truly successful, a competent mother of the bride doesn't really order people about so much as encourages them. Her years of motherhood and life experience have taught her three things. First, that most people are idiots and unreliable. Second, that most of her family are idiots and unreliable. Finally, that spouting orders only confuses the idiots, whether they be family, catering staff, or even the DJ.

On the day of the wedding, most fathers of the bride actually believe they're in control of the proceedings.

They think what's really needed is for the wedding party to behave like a football team, with everyone pulling together. Fathers are prone to this delusion, stressed or not. Most expect the highest adulation, numerous "thank yous" during the toasting, and SportsCenter highlights, courtesy of the wedding videographer, for their leadership, which in reality amounted to little more than toweling off the game balls before kickoff.

But the mother remembers what the father forgets—you have a team of idiots.

There's no professionalism in your family, and everyone makes the team. Blind Aunt Mavis can't be placed on waivers for screwing up the flower arrangements. A winning team is meticulously built over the course of numerous seasons, not at the rehearsal dinner. Those with small springs are inevitably left as chaff on the playing field to serve as compost.

The groomsmen have their own game plan in mind and are usually getting loaded before the wedding even begins. Yes, after a few cold ones, many of these former high school BMOCs will throw away the wedding playbook altogether in favor of more attractive strategies, which involve figuring out which bridesmaid is the hottest or the easiest or both. After a few more barley pops, they're no longer sober enough to get a bag of ice. I've seen far too many wedding-party processionals with staggering groomsmen. Useless.

The bridesmaids manage to stay sober enough and are generally excited to be suiting up for the game. But here the problem is strictly with the uniform and equipment. Most of these fine ladies are smart, hardy folks, but they insist on dressing like strippers. Most wear heels more appropriately reserved for a red-light district than a wedding. I've witnessed processions of bridesmaids aerate acres of open field at outdoor weddings with nothing more than their five-inch heels. Their dresses are usually ill-fitting and impractical. The colors eggplant, tomato, and green pepper should never be needed to describe a bridesmaid dress.

Ninety percent of bridesmaids plan to lose weight for the big day. But simply telling the bride eight months before the wedding that you're a size ten doesn't make you a size ten, especially if your closet is full of size-fourteen dresses. Needless to say, the weight is not lost, the dress does not fit, and the result is a parade of overstuffed, pear-shaped women the color of nightshade vegetables eagerly looking for a dish of baked rigatoni punching holes in the lawn with their idiotic footwear.

One of the bigger challenges are the former neighbors. These are people expecting to be invited to the wedding just by virtue of the fact that you once lived next to them for six months in the 1980s. These people insist on inviting themselves to the wedding in order to see their little Victoria march down the aisle. Bastards.

Family, like clichés, are harmless for the most part. I once read an inspirational quote on a pizza-box-sized wedding invitation which read "Every family has a story to tell, welcome to ours." (If your invitation was on a pizza box, maybe there's quite a bit to tell.) This brings me back to the Psych 202 treatise. As the nonstoned may remember, pathology exists within each of us, and stress can bring out the abnormal proclivities we try to hide from others.

In the case of family, it's no different. In much the

same way that we keep our inner selves hidden, so too our dark family secrets. As a precaution, most parents will first slowly ease the new boyfriend or girlfriend in with the lighter fare of their family's dysfunction. This is a tenuous prospect.

Most future in-laws indoctrinate prospective family members in stages. It usually begins with idle banter. Parents might start saying things like, "It's true that Cindy's brother is in special education, he's just a little slow, but we're expecting him to really excel in the vocational arts." Or that her truck-driving aunt, now goes by the handle "Big Fred." They build intimacy by divulging secrets that are passed off casually as if they were comments about the weather or the limitless culinary uses of asparagus and pesto.

But these are merely hors d'oeuvres. The salad will include references to the irreverent cross-dressing Uncle David, what a jokester, and the bride's grandmother who was a member of the Manson Family in the 1960s. Most parents seem determined to take the future family member at least as far as the main course, which stirs even darker waters, better left undisturbed. But even with all this courteous sharing, most walk down the aisle having skipped dessert, aware of only half the story.

I stayed with my wife after learning her family history because my own family's dysfunction is as deep and mysterious as the Mariana Trench. My wife's family history was a mere anglerfish by comparison. When addressing my family secrets to my future partner, I skipped dinner altogether and opted for brunch. Pesto or asparagus omelets, anyone?

Relatives are problematic because they're kith and kin

and you cannot fire them. They're members of your team, and you must take the field, aerated or not, with the players that you have. Also, family you've never met (and you never wanted to meet) tend to show up in full display at weddings. Like peacocks, they strut around greeting everyone yet knowing no one, providing colorful behavioral displays hinting at deeply recessive genes and winking at evolutionary failures.

Many families are nothing more than neurological disasters waiting to change from fluid to airborne pathogens.

To be fair, most of the mothers of the bride that I've worked with prove to be sane, sober people, with just an inkling of chronic worry and a chance of nagging. They navigate the treacherous waters of family, idiots, and guests with a feminine resilience unknown to the world of men. Pride is for men. For them, all goes well, providing of course they have at least a medium or better spring. But when mother has a small spring and is paying for and planning the wedding, in the presence of unstable family alchemy, that's when the show begins. Enter Mommy Dearest. There were warning signs. A mismatch between the bride's expectations and those of the mother, for starters. Janie wanted a small wedding of a hundred guests, while her mother was determined to have two or three times that amount.

According to Mommy Dearest, her wedding in 1975 was a small and intimate affair. Whenever I hear the words "small" and "intimate" used in the same sentence to describe a wedding, it's not hard to figure out the subtext. Her real honeymoon was in 1974, not 1975, when little

Janie was conceived in a '65 Ford Mustang with an unprepared drone she would later call "father".

A baby bump started showing during the second trimester, before her parents could get the pastor to allow the couple to be married in the church, let alone allow the bride to wear white. Growing up in a religious household I learned that any Lutheran congregation worth its commandments can easily spot the best disguised baby bump.

Mommy Dearest insists that her daughter just doesn't know what she wants. "You know how it is," she says. Yes, I'm afraid I do. The guest list is doubled, by the mother's choosing, which increases tenfold the number of idiots attending.

The meltdowns. Their dresses may have cost upwards of several thousand dollars apiece, but I've witnessed mothers and daughters engage in MMA-style combat prior to the exchange of nuptials. Every bride exhibits a few vague anxieties about getting married prior to taking her father's arm for the trip down the aisle, but doubt? Mommy Dearest will hear nothing of this. "I've already paid the caterer and the hall rental and a deposit to that pathetic, old-looking DJ. So you're going to get out there and get married, do you hear me? I've spent too much and traveled to hell and back for you, so you'll not be ruining our special day."

They often bring out the tarot deck of guilt cards. "You took the milk from my breast and continued to take, didn't you? Ballet lessons and cheer camps. Your father and I paid for your private liberal-arts college, despite your 2.3 GPA. So dry your eyes, sweetie, and get out there before I really give you something to cry about." After a final kick in the trousseau, the bride almost always acquiesces, and seven months later little Horace is born with course, red hair protruding from each ear canal. Welcome to the family.

Blood being thicker than wine, Mommy Dearest will start to blame nonfamily members for anything that goes wrong. For example, if Uncle David trips on his way to the buffet it was due to the caterer's incompetence because they set up the buffet in the wrong location. She conveniently forgets about the seven barley pops that Uncle David drank with the groomsmen prior to the wedding. He may be falling down drunk, but that hot plate had no business being anywhere near an electrical outlet, and any good tray of rigatoni should be able to withstand the occasional collision with a drunken guest or bridesmaid dressed like an eggplant.

The mothers begin asking me to make more and more announcements pertaining to frivolous things. If the attendees haven't signed the guest book by now I seriously doubt making a twentieth announcement is going to do any damn good. They rush up screaming for me to play something different because nobody's dancing. My medium spring absorbs the shock, and I respond in a level, professional tone that I'll start picking it up once the guests have finished their salads. Most guests find it difficult to dance the electric slide or macarena while eating a large plate of pasta.

As the DJ, you should expect that some of these mothers will become fixated on you and monitor everything you say or play. When not demeaning you, these same women will cozy up to make comments like "I don't think you should play 'Ruby' by Kenny Rogers. Some of our veterans may be offended. Uncle David was in that terrible war, and look what happened to him." Later, if there's a lull in the dancing, she'll demand a new song. "Can't you see nobody's dancing? Play something else now, the guests are leaving, can't you see that the guests are leaving? Are you high?" I tighten my spring down a second turn. It wouldn't do either of us any good to point out that I'm playing the songs off her own playlist.

These women also become obsessed with the idea that everybody at the reception depart with a hideous centerpiece as a memento. Without exception, the centerpieces are ugly, heavy, full of water, and make one think they're at a cemetery. Most are thrown out at the first rest stop on the way home. The ugliness of the centerpieces is inversely correlated to the physical attractiveness of the couple. This holds true to what I've always believed, that beautiful people tend to do ugly things.

The most disastrous breakdown of any Mommy Dearest I've ever witnessed occurred during a summer wedding in 2007. It was a mid-August, outdoor ceremony set for two o'clock, reception to follow in the 105-degree heat. The cake people had placed the cake in the shade under a tent awning two hours prior. It was a monster three-layer and covered more than half of the folding table. Around that same time four kegs of beer were dropped off by the beer people. Three of the kegs were ushered off to the beer garden by the groomsmen and placed in sixty-gallon garbage cans filled with ice. Mmmm, beer. Somebody showed up with the taps, and the first keg was already being drained by the groomsmen an hour before the ceremony.

The forgotten keg was left alone in the sun across from my DJ table. The best man passed by, Solo drinking cup in hand, and I pointed out that someone might want to put the forgotten keg undercover, so the beer could stay cold. He looked at me. He looked at the keg. He walked away finishing his beer. I could guess his best-man speech in about three hours would include the phrase "what happens in Vegas stays in Vegas" as well as the word "cojones." I quickly forgot about the keg as I had to do a second DJ setup for the ceremony in the vineyard several hundred feet away. When I returned to start the reception forty minutes later, I noticed that the keg of beer was now wrapped in black plastic and elegantly secured with bungee cords. The reception started, the buffet was opened, and the music played.

All through the reception Mommy Dearest was in everyone's ear. I noticed that she was now nagging, not encouraging, the family and guests to comply with her wedding agenda. She confided in me that she'd had it with both the photographer and wedding planner. I agreed with her that most of the blame should be placed on the catering staff.

Later, she pulled me aside, assuring me that she was sorry I'd had such poor prospects in my life that I'd ended up becoming a DJ but that she thought I was doing an okay job for an older person. She was so sincere that I didn't have the heart to tell her that DJing was my side job and that I had a master's degree. Some of the guests were beginning to leave so I suggested we move on to the cake cutting.

I made the necessary announcements and added that the bridal party and guests needed to be front and center, as we were cutting the cake in about ten minutes. While the tables were being cleared I noticed the keg of beer still sitting in the sun, wrapped in black plastic. The inebriated groomsmen began tapping the keg with none of them considering the heat. The temperature of the beer was somewhere near boiling. The best man inadvertently pushed down on the spring-loaded ball valve and received a scalding beer facial. What followed would have given the Three Stooges, Laurel and Hardy, and Buster Keaton a collective run for their money.

Groomsman One stumbled back into Groomsman Two, who backed into Groomsman Three, who fell back onto the already-melting cake. The cake table collapsed, Groomsman Three went down, and the cake slid on top of Groomsmen Two and Three. Then Groomsman One fell forward and took a second beer facial, and knocked the tap off the keg.

A geyser of barley pop reminiscent of Old Faithful was sent gushing forty feet into the midafternoon sky. Sixteen gallons vaporized in seven seconds. The beer rainbow was breathtaking, a rhapsody in brew. The bridal party and guests and what was left of the cake were soaked with hot-tub temperature beer. As the last of the beer fell from the sky, the rainbow collapsed in upon itself like a black hole, pulling Mommy Dearest into a maelstrom of insanity.

Everyone at the wedding began laughing. But Mommy Dearest didn't laugh. She stood there sheeted in beer, like Carrie during the fiery prom scene.

Not possessing any psychokinetic powers, Mommy Dearest looked around for someone to blame for what had happened: me, the idiots, Uncle David, the groomsmen, the eggplants. But it was a no-go. Her spring had sprung.

Mommy Dearest screamed before falling to the beer-battered lawn in spasmodic contortions. She went motionless after several moments and was dragged away by a groomsman covered in cake and an eggplant sautéed in beer.

I made an announcement later, at the bride's request, explaining that her mother had experienced a case of sunstroke and wouldn't be returning but that we were all welcome to stay. Sunstroke? Maybe. Small spring? Definitely. I threw out Mommy Dearest's playlist. Another keg was tapped without a rainbow connection, and the party began in earnest. A good time was had by all.

There exists a cliché that if you want to know what your bride will look like as she ages, look at her mother. This may be true. However, experience has taught me that while all things fade over time, the crazy never does. If your mother-in-law is a Mommy Dearest, crazy will be in your future long past the wedding day.

I ran into the same Mommy Dearest, the bride, and her family at another wedding a year later. At the reception, I overheard Mommy Dearest describe over and over again how funny the exploding keg had been. All things fade over time, but not the crazy.

GROOM UP!

I N THE OLD days, things were simple. A bridal show was called a wedding expo. Wedding expos only contained wedding stuff. A stroll down wedding yesteryear would reveal only the necessities of matrimony. This was what we in the business called the bridal industrial complex. There were vendors displaying wedding cakes, wedding dresses, and tuxedo rentals. This was before online printing and Grammarly. Some of the booths would be occupied by stationers. They were a most serious group, as serious people are often the best spellers. They were there to print wedding announcements, envelopes, and RSVP cards, always with correct spelling and grammar, guaranteed. Caterers would give samples of tasty hors d'oeuvres. What better way to gain the business of the fickle couple than by consoling the stomach before pillaging the wallet? And we must not forget the florists.

Today, there is only the bridal show, a mandatory circus of the bizarre for the unsuspecting bride and groom. No longer does the couple have the luxury of planning just their special day. Now the push is for cradle to grave exploitation. Any business or vendor with a deposit fee can secure a booth or corner table and solicit with impunity.

I felt the same way about these non sequitur vendors

as I did about The Others on the television series Lost. The Others were more interesting when they were in the periphery, but quickly lost their charm when placed front and center in comparison to the Dharma Initiative and the smoke monster. A walk through a modern bridal show today is, to put it modestly, eclectic.

At my last bridal show I was located on row C, booth space 44. Along my row, I observed that one could get a massage, talk to a lawyer about legal planning and prenups, get the ins and outs on cleansing from Doc Colonic, and buy a cake from the Have Your Cake and Eat it Too bakery. I could also purchase term life insurance, buy flowers, and sign up for a sultry bridal shower lingerie party.

I must admit to feeling slightly red-faced when walking past booth space 43, The Lovey Dovey Lingerie Emporium, specializing in adult toys. They had set up a most sensuous display. The double booth space displayed male and female mannequins wearing sexy outfits.

All the display mannequins had exaggerated features and proportions. The female forms were large-breasted and thin-waisted, with the curviest behinds you never see in nature. The male model (there was only one) was nude except for a black G-string sporting a white bow tie. This randy groom-mannequin resembled a young George Clooney after six months of human growth hormone and thirteen months of CrossFit. The banner stretching over the top of their booth really said it all: "To love another, we must first come to love ourselves." I believe this was their business plan. They also had a drawing for a free vibrator. Ooh la la.

A happy unmarried couple could walk down one side

of Row C and sample some cake, look at flowers, and enter to win a free vibrator. If having reached the end of Row C, the groom realizes that the cake sample he ate contained almond paste not disclosed clearly to the public in compliance with city ordinance number 42, he could walk right down the other side and talk to a lawyer about suing the Have Your Cake and Eat it Too bakery for undisclosed almond paste poisoning; then he could get a massage to stay calm while waiting for the paramedics, and buy term life insurance before it's too late. Depending on the outcome, the justice of the peace and the cemetery plot people were over on row E, next to the kettle corn. One stop shopping.

I would undertake two bridal shows a year to help fill out my DJ calendar. The cost would run about 750 dollars a day, depending on booth size and show location. The larger shows could run over 1000 dollars a day. If I could secure at least two weddings over a weekend, I broke even. Also, all the show vendors would get a list of the attendees' emails and phone numbers. If you worked the list you could usually get another five weddings. These lists allowed the DJ and the cemetery plot people to stalk the happy couple up to the day of their wedding and, in some cases, long after.

The bridal show opened at 9:00AM. I was exhausted from a wedding the previous night. Five hours of sleep was standard since the baby was born, but this Saturday morning was especially hard. In the morning mirror I was forty, looking every bit of sixty. Not the best look for winning over twenty-something couples in search of a young, energetic Party Maker Jam Master.

My wife offered me some of her under-eye concealer

to cover up my late night. I thanked her for her thoughtfulness but declined. The wedding show was in the city. People still got beat up for wearing concealer downtown. I would use the "I've seen it all before, been through one too many weddings" staff sergeant approach. I would be grizzled and humorous. I would play up my late night and years of experience.

The bridal show opened like the invasion of Normandy, with 500 brides trying to secure their section of the matrimonial beachhead. They stormed into the giant ballroom room at a dead run. The future grooms were no match for their wives-to-be and fell behind. When it comes to singularity of purpose, a spawning salmon has nothing on a motivated bride. Some of the future grooms trailed in, looking lost, many oblivious to the fact they were getting married despite being at a bridal show. I fear that some may have actually lost their future wives during the invasion.

After fifteen minutes, the crowd began trickling down Row C. We vendors were smiling pleasantly, waiting for the chance to give our first pitch of the day. Julian, one of the masseuses, had taken off his windbreaker jacket to reveal bulging biceps and a six-pack visible through his white t-shirt. The logo over his left, very pronounced, pectoral muscle listed the name of the company as Magic Hands Massage. His female co-masseuse, Porsche, had also stripped down to reveal tight leggings and an ornately stylish sports bra printed with the company logo. Doc Colonic was at the ready to distribute brochures listing the ins and outs of his services.

But all the brochures, biceps, and bras in the world could not compete with the spectacle that was Lovey

Dovey. Couples were being drawn in by the raw sensuality of the display like moths to a bug zapper, or maybe the way women get with shoes. Our cash-rich future clients were walking past our booths and going straight to Lovey Dovey. Several couples did stop to take a free cake sample before giddily sashaying over to fondle the "Iron Mike Love Pistol."

A couple would arrive at Lovey Dovey and immediately be asked to take a five-question sexual compatibility test. They were assigned one of four colors based on their responses. Glenda, the owner, would then proceed to probe the couple for more intimate details.

If you were a red, you liked spontaneous sex, surprises, and numerous positions during coitus. If you were a blue, you were into planned destination-orientated romantic encounters like, say, going to Fiji. Also, the blues tended to prefer only one or two sexual positions during coitus. The greens were somewhere in the middle. This group was somewhat spontaneous, liked two to three positions, was less adventuresome with other forms of sex play, but they also had the highest likelihood of achieving climax. The yellows just liked it rough.

Most of the brides were self-reported reds, the spontaneous sex group. After my son was born 6 months ago, all sex was spontaneous. As for positions? Nodding off while diapering the baby had become a favorite.

Glenda, that vixen, talked about sex and answered questions about sex all morning long. I thought about how some people have an amazing talent to talk to anyone about anything. Yep. How often the bride achieved climax on her own, as opposed to with her partner, was a topic of frequent discourse. I wondered how long I could stand around asking people about their respective percentages in reaching climax without getting punched or arrested.

Couples that stopped at the Lovey Dovey booth would take the sex quiz and then put in a few tickets for the free vibrator drawing. Most stayed for about fifteen minutes. Often couples would walk away from Lovey Dovey with a slight blush on their rosy faces, sometimes smiles of satisfaction, or grins of anticipation. One couple disappeared into a unisex restroom.

Most couples stepping away from the booth, however, were whisked back to the stark reality of the bridal industrial complex too quickly. The adjustment from reflecting upon the benefits of the "Manskin" attachment to your future husband's scrotum to choosing your cake frosting can be rather daunting. And transitioning from a sensual blue honeymoon romantic destination getaway, to hiring a sixty-year-old looking DJ is obviously way too much to ask of anyone.

No one was stopping by booth number 44, Row C. I was going to need a strategy to put them at ease after their encounter with Lovey Dovey if I wanted to solicit with impunity.

Strategy one: as the couple was leaving, I would attempt to catch their gaze and offer my "I've seen it all before" smile with a knowing head nod, reminiscent of a bus driver welcoming a passenger onboard. Maybe I would peel up my lip to flash a few pearly teeth, closing to a grin.

The first couple took one look at this geriatric nodding bus driver and hurried in the opposite direction to see Doc Colonic about a cleanse. Next, a future groom sauntered over, bride in tow, to check out my display. He was probably taken in by my double nod, followed by a smirk. I had overheard the couple talking to Glenda about wanting to "open up" their relationship. He may have thought my double nod was a go-ahead for a future three-way. There had to be a better way to break the sensual tension.

Strategy two: humor. Any couple that had just entered a drawing for a free vibrator must have a sense of humor. For my first attempt I quipped, "I see you're starting the honeymoon before the wedding," without realizing that the future bride was about seventeen years old and six months pregnant. The groom was around eighteen and just beginning to clue into the fact that he was at a bridal show. His mother was not amused. After an awkward silence, I handed the groom a brochure.

To the next blushing couple, I asked, "You're going to want a DJ to go with that?" They looked at me, then at the vibrator, then at each other, before shaking their heads in a collective no. I wasn't getting any weddings on the books, but I did get my second rejection for a three-way before noon, a first for me. I decided to dial down my sales pitch. I handed them my brochure and said "Got a DJ?" Bingo.

Glenda, that vixen, asked me how I was doing. She told me that Lovey Dovey had already booked ten brides for their bridal show lingerie extravaganza parties. Glenda looked around coyly, not wanting to divulge her trade secrets to any lingering brides. This is how intimacy is created between vendors in the bridal industrial complex. She said the key to boosting sales was getting everyone drunk at the bridal shower. Also, lingerie was where she made her highest profit although her sales of adult toys had paid for her vacation home last year.

I lied and told her I was also doing well, considering my late night. I failed to mention the disruption her free vibrator giveaway was having on my business. She was sympathetic and said that she had a vitamin sample from a previous show that might help. She returned with a blue tea bag-sized packet and a banana-flavored condom. I opened my wallet. She told me they were on the house.

I could use a boost; my quad espresso had done nothing. In the first half hour of the two-day show, I had already established myself as a perverted sixty-year-old looking staff sergeant driving a transit bus, pretending to be a DJ, and nodding at young couples trying to get into three-ways. Not a good look for a forty-year-old DJ.

The packet was labeled "Groom UP" and "not for resale" was printed in tiny letters below the title. The flipside listed ingredients in an even smaller font. Under "usage" was printed proudly and in bold: "To increase stamina."

When I was four years old, I remember seeing a TV commercial for a breakfast cereal. It featured a Native American man, dressed in the fashion of the Plains Indians, running across the grasslands chasing some buffalo. The narrator described how the cereal contained magnesium and thiamine to increase stamina.

To this day, when I hear the word "stamina" I think of real Plains Indians chasing buffalo. I needed a little stamina. If the Native American warrior without a horse could catch a buffalo, how many wedding couples could I run down and capture? That commercial ran for about a year, usually between episodes of H.R. Pufnstuf and

The Bugaloos. Question: thinking back, as an adult, what were 1960s TV executives smoking?

Groom UP contained numerous herbs I had never heard of, with lots of "weed" this, or "wort" that, but no thiamine or magnesium. Had 1960s television been a lie? I was frightening away potential clients and figured I needed all the help I could get. I swallowed both capsules.

As the second hour of the show came and went I felt the first wave of manly renewal wash over me. My new KISS (keep it simple stupid) strategy was working famously. I was finally making some cash despite the slow start. Seize the day? Hell, my Indian friend and I would be chasing down entire herds of buffalo if this kept up.

I was taking a deposit from a couple when I felt something more than the usual excitement of locking in a customer. The stamina in the pills had little to do with chasing buffalo. No, taking Groom UP apparently encouraged one to participate in physical activity of a horizontal sort. I did feel revitalized, though. I felt twenty and looked forty. Below the waist, I had the strength of 100 men. My thinking and clarity of vision were now crystalline.

After the couple departed, I was left standing alone behind my thirty-two-inch-tall display table wearing thirty-four-inch inseam slacks. Parts of me were becoming self-aware. Do I commit to the right or the left? Democrat or Republican? Being a Libertarian, I settled on limited government and upholding personal freedoms and held my brochures proudly in the center.

My wife had something that I badly needed. And I had a plan. I would simply call her and explain the situation, without panting. In this flight of fantasy, my wife would call her mother who would immediately drive over to watch our sleeping child. After driving the twelve miles to the bridal show at 125 mph in her Ford Escort, my wife would park in the thirty-minute load/unload zone. I would meet her there with a blanket. Problem solved.

I also noticed the surprising amount of space under my skirted banquet table. We could both fit, if the thirty-minute zone was too impersonal. I would pretend to show her the booth and both of us would discreetly disappear under the table. We had done it before at the Boat Show. I would even pay.

If we needed assistance, Glenda from Lovey Dovey, I am sure, would be willing to reach across the aisle if we developed any problems due to our coital incompatibility. I realized while listening to Glenda that my wife was a blue, and myself? Canary yellow. I picked up my phone to call home. Ring, ring, ring . . . nothing.

Soon I began to appreciate how attractive everyone really was. Julian, Porsche, Doc Colonic, the married couple from Have Your Cake and Eat it Too. Imagine yourself at forty years of age and for the first time discovering the truly deep erotic draw of purchasing term life insurance. It occurred to me that maybe the Indian from the commercial was chasing more than buffalo. Ring, ring, ring . . . nothing.

The Lovey Dovey mannequins caught my eye. They were winking at me in a secret knowing way, they knew I was a yellow. My Indian friend and I would run across the plains of fortune. I would be the great white buffalo.

Normally fashion shows are held on the main stage, in the center of the ballroom. But this year was different.

The models would be walking down the individual rows showcasing the latest bridal fashions.

First came the wedding dresses. Beautiful models, beautiful brides, all so good looking. Corset-style wedding dresses were all the rage at the time. My favorite. Then came the grooms and groomsmen in their tuxes. Less appealing, but also attractive. Father of the bride was next. Even the bridesmaids in their silly strapless dresses were kind of hot. It was a buffet of beauty. All I needed to do was reach across my display table.

But there was more. The models had changed into destination fashions for Fiji.

Down Row C came these same sexy ladies, now donning flowery and revealing dresses with slits to the waist, with feathered hair falling loose around their shoulders like it would on a bedroom pillow. So soft. Then came the men sporting polo shirts with khakis or cargo shorts. Meh. Meanwhile, other models had changed into revealing swimwear. Oh yes. Out came the colorful one-piece numbers followed by enchantresses wearing Brazilian string bikinis. Aye, Caramba!

The show had climaxed, or so I thought. But no. There was an encore. A bridal lingerie show courtesy of Lovey Dovey. Brazen bridal babes began a beguiling blockade in brocaded bustiers for the wedding, and the honeymoon to come. Even the mother of the bride had lingerie that was especially made for her.

Apparently, while Daughter was away on her red-meets-blue, four-position coitus, three-day, three-way, destination sex-safari, old Mom was going to play, and slip into something more comfortable for her own yellow-on-yellow, sex fest with Father. Now that is marketing. Stay focused, I thought. Catch the buffalo. Catch the buffalo.

After the fashion show, I continued to man my post. I was a virile and vivacious Party Maker Jam Master Supreme. Ten weddings were on the books with deposits. My Indian friend was with me in spirit, "Go, great white buffalo!" he chanted in the language of the Sioux. I bounced from couple to couple, like a rubber ball, dispensing wedding wisdom and brochures. Everyone was nodding now. This would be my best bridal show ever if only I could find a way to cage the elephant.

During a lull, I walked three booths down. The man sitting in front of this particular display was named Richard. He was a very serious looking man, probably a former stationer, definitely a good speller. Dick was one of the partners of the firm Knob, Wood, Tally, Wacker, and Johnson. He asked me how he could help. I explained that he already had, and walked away, taking one of his business cards. Nothing kills an erection like a lawyer.

I was able to complete the bridal show and sign a record fifteen weddings, most with cash deposits. I returned home to my wife with a renewed energy for life. She was upstairs nodding off after diapering. A good time was had by all, several times. The result: an eight-pound love child nine months later, special thanks to Glenda at Lovey Dovey.

TRYING TO CATCH THE DELUGE
IN A PAPER CUP

JANUARY 1, 2000, it would all be over. According to the musical recording artist Prince, two thousand zero zero, party over, oops, out of time. All I remember about 1999 was a summer wedding season which started in February and continued robustly through November. Apparently large numbers of couples wanted to be joined for eternity before facing the uncertain future. If the world was going to hell it was better to share it with someone you loved. Isn't that what marriage is all about? Single people would feel just as awkward and incomplete in Hades, as they did in everyday life. Rightly so.

December 1998 came in with a blizzard of corporate Christmas parties. You remember those? People got together to share a little Christmas cheer, a lot of booze, and embarrassing photos the following Monday. An attempt by the management team and HR at "trust building." After all, there's nothing like a cup of mulled wine or a quadruple vodka in December to take the edge off the pink slips coming in January. People believed in Christmas parties, like I did in Tinkerbell in the Disney classic *Peter Pan*; I clapped. In the 1990s, people weren't as cynical as they are today. We still wanted to believe in Bigfoot, Santa Claus, and a monogamous president.

1999 started eventfully for me. At a bridal show in

January I booked a record twenty weddings in a two-day period. The conception of my second son occurred the same weekend following herbally enhanced coitus. My compliments to Man Up and the Lovey Dovey Lingerie Emporium. Ooh la la.

This may have been the year of the cataclysm, but it was also the year of the double mocha. I'd been a flowery, light-in-the-loafers, triple-vanilla-latte guy all through the late '80s. In 1990, I got my first real job, with little time for light or loafers. I became a straight-black-coffee guy. No cream, no sugar. It's true what they say, once you go black, you never go back. I never did.

Espresso stands were everywhere, and it seemed that the double mocha was the preferred choice of newly converted espresso aficionados. My first experience with a double mocha, however, was also my last.

During a rainy week in late January, I went downtown with my friend Fred to look at guitars. This was a welcomed and novel outing for me but commonplace for Fred. Apparently, when one gets excellent at playing the guitar, one begins to obsess about guitars and notice the individual nuances and intricacies of every instrument. My wife was a lot like Fred, only with footwear. Although a musician and a shoe wearer myself, I was never willing to dedicate the study necessary on any instrument, or quality footwear to gain professional status. I found it easier to hang out with musical prodigies and live vicariously while wearing high-top Converse All Stars.

After entering the music store, we met sales associate "Frip." He was being very attentive and helpful, at first. He even tried to impress us with poorly executed versions of Cheap Trick covers. That's before the guys from

Queensryche came in. From the moment the local rock gods honored us common folk with a visit, the entire store went over to kiss their heavy metal asses. Before puckering, Frip yanked the guitar Fred was playing from his hands midsolo to show it to the rock royalty.

While the hard rock veterans smoked behind the building with the sales staff, Fred and I might have stolen a hundred guitars and cleaned out all three cash registers. We both could have experienced seizures, with no one in the store taking notice to call an ambulance. A year later the store closed due to slumping sales and theft. Little wonder.

In the 1980s, I knew two fellow high school students who used to fake seizures for fun. These guys would pretend to shop at a crowded department store before one of them would fall to the ground giving an Oscar-worthy performance. The act would include grabbing the feet of those around him and uttering inarticulate profanity. This was followed by lots of spitting and drooling.

His cohort would tell everyone to stand back and inform the growing crowd that his friend was having a diabetic seizure due to low blood sugar. He'd pretend to check the friend's vital signs before pulling out a packet of sugar and pouring the contents into the victim's mouth. His seizing accomplice would begin blinking erratically and slowly return to consciousness. The Good Samaritan would help his cohort to his feet to the applause of the crowd. Often, they were given money by older couples, so the poor boy could get some food in his stomach.

They preferred performing in JCPenney stores. The lower- and middle-class patrons were more compassionate and genuinely concerned. They faked a seizure in an exclusive department store downtown and nobody stopped. The upper-class clientele remained nonchalant, stepping over the convulsing body. If you touched these customers' shoes, you'd be severely reminded that those were $500 Guccis you were soiling, and if you didn't let go you'd have more than a seizure to worry about.

The clerks, per their extensive training, would relay the company's zero-tolerance policy for drooling and inarticulate swearing. Smiling, they'd suggest you might be happier shopping at Sears or a JCPenney. Those experiencing seizures and drooling would surely be welcome there.

Their swan song occurred in a Macy's. After one of them had collapsed to the floor, a trauma nurse who happened to be shopping during her lunch break came to the victim's aide. From her years of experience in the emergency room, she knew at a glance that his stylized seizure was due to epilepsy and immediately called for an ambulance on her walkie-talkie. She was gravely concerned that the victim's inarticulate swearing and overly abundant drooling was a clear sign of a concussion acquired after falling. In a moment of panic, both thespians broke the fourth wall and quit the scene, exiting stage right at a full sprint. They hid inside an Orange Julius until the mall closed.

Having been dissed by "Frip" and the music-store guys, we both needed a coffee. Being close to an upper-class, seizure-discerning, no-drooling department store downtown with their own espresso shop, we went in. Following Fred's lead, I ordered a double venti, double mocha with whip. I received a huge paper cup filled with forty ounces of coffee, milk, chocolate, and whip. All for $4.99. It wasn't just coffee anymore.

Fred said he needed to take a pee. This was not surprising as he'd been a frequent urinator during the five years I'd known him. But of late, I'd noticed a marked increase in frequency. Uncharacteristically, Fred had started avoiding social urinating experiences in favor of single-stall eliminations. I began to suspect that Fred's change from social urinator to the antisocial was merely a reflection of our fading friendship. After talking with others in our circle, though, I came to believe that his emotional withdrawal from those around him was due to something far deeper. Tapeworms. His overactive bladder was a clear symptom of parasitic intestinal inflammation.

Always the supportive friend, never the BFF, I knew to stay silent. Any attempt to increase intimacy on my part might be viewed as an effort to control and jeopardize the marginal relationship to which I continued to cling. As was often the case, we concluded our emotional interaction with a passionless stare into the dark necessities of each other's souls. I'd once again wear the mask and play the part of the "good friend" while stifling tears. Regardless, Fred needed to pee.

Being a social urinator myself, I went along for support. We entered the large restroom, mochas in hand. The restroom was packed with frequent, lunchtime, and social urinators. Being taller than Fred, I took the last open urinal per prevailing West Coast restroom etiquette. Fred would have to accept his lower station and access the stall closest to the sinks. I started to go, then Fred let go.

A wave of thick, brown, milky goo exploded from

inside the stall and across the restroom floor behind me. Some creamier bits managed to clear the top of the stall and splattered on the urinal in front of me. Like a spawning salmon confronting a Kodiak bear, I was stopped midstream. The scene became grizzly.

The lunchtime urinators pulled up their pants and pranced around like they were wearing high-heeled shoes to avoid the infectious goo. Many of these men, I'm sure, were brave souls willing to face anything Y2K, the World Trade Organization (WTO), or zombies. But diarrhea on a cataclysmic scale such as this was too much for anyone.

The social urinators having little stomach for bodily functions in general, let alone diarrhea, ran out of the restroom with their pants around their ankles. Even the professional urinators fled in terror, most half-zipped, screaming that the end times were upon us.

Then, all was still. Fred was dead. That was a certainty. No one could void that much liquid and live. What would I say at his eulogy? I already knew what the autopsy would show—death by mischievous misadventure. Tapeworms. Then I heard a stirring and what may have been a whisper. Make it go away, make it all go away. If alive, Fred would need help cleaning up. But all friendships have limitations, right? Then I heard his familiar voice: "I knocked over my mocha." He kicked the empty cup out from under the stall.

He laughed. I laughed. The two of us laughed the way we used to laugh together during that carefree first year. My salmon again found its stream. Hope does spring eternal. I finished my business as Fred wiped himself off with paper towels. He looked relatively unscathed, considering. I left my double mocha unviolated on the top of the urinal. Back to black coffee for me. As we were leaving the restroom we passed a cleaning crew of eight dressed in hazmat suits.

In February 1999, when Pluto was still a planet, a beloved president nicknamed Slick Willy was acquitted from impeachment. I also DJ'd my first *Groundhog Day* (the movie) theme party. The location was at an old Eagles Hall. It didn't pay a lot. But any cash in February is welcome, and any "novelty" is appreciated after your three hundredth wedding. Darren, the organizer, was hoping for a Comic Con type of turnout.

Out of the hundred guests that showed, only half came in costume. The men mostly dressed like Bill Murray and the ladies like groundhogs. One guy showed up dressed like Larry the Cameraman, played by Chris Elliott. He went around filming the event live with his camcorder. One of the couples in attendance looked like professional groundhogs. They were wearing expensive costumes, covered from snout to tail.

The group took advantage of the happy-hour drink specials with most getting slammed before the buffet opened. Later, Darren took the microphone to welcome everyone to his first annual *Groundhog Day* celebration. He wasn't the best of public speakers but managed several spot-on Bill Murray impersonations. His groundhog noises, though, were reminiscent of the habitually mating guinea pigs my sister used to breed in our basement. Eerie.

After the dancing started, the groundhog couple really got into the music and started going front to back and riding each other's legs. It was cute at first, then just plain weird as they started rubbing their pointy groundhog tails between the legs of the other dancers. If they hadn't been wearing cute costumes they probably would've been arrested.

Watching the horny rodents on the dance floor made me think of the song "Muskrat Love" recorded by America. I made out with Julie Morgan to this song in junior high. Looking at the groundhog couple mounting each other, and just about everyone else, pretty much killed the memory. At midnight, I packed it up fast. I wasn't waiting around to see if the groundhogs would see their shadows or not.

March came in like a lion with three weddings that first weekend. I also got an opportunity to DJ a Saint Patrick's Day celebration at a Chinese restaurant. The restaurant staff all dressed like leprechauns. The crowd was mostly Russian immigrants. No matter, the buffet was amazing with sweet-and-sour pork, fried rice, and Peking duck nestled between steaming pans of boiled potatoes and corned beef with cabbage.

The restaurant was called the Rickshaw. This had been a regular venue for up-and-coming hard rock and metal bands in the 1980s. My old band had played our first paying show there. The compensation was lousy, but the band could eat and drink for free, and nobody checked ID. The stage was big and had a lot of lights. Playing there left you hopeful that you might someday make it big. Well, here I was, once again, but what of the band?

With April showers came wedding dollars for this DJ. After working the contact list from the bridal show in January, I now had an additional fifteen weddings on the books. Backstreet Boys released their new Album *Millen-*

nium. Not really my style of music, but the three singles got a lot of airplay. My motto: Always play what the bride pays. May was busy with consultations for weddings in June and July.

I met one couple at a wine bar in early June to draw up their one-of-a-kind, share-our-special-day wedding agenda. I was tasting. They were drinking wine out of water glasses. Later in the month when I showed up to play their wedding reception, they had no idea who I was. I've had couples get hammered at the wedding reception and not remember me leaving, but not remembering our initial meeting was a first.

A memorable wedding in July was country themed and out on a twenty-five-acre family homestead. The bridal party was dressed in formal attire with the accoutrement of cowboy hats and boots. After setting up my equipment, I played a varied selection of background music and some of the couple's requests.

To my right, I saw a tall, thin woman dressed conservatively in a long dress. She was having considerable difficulty walking down the grassy slope to meet up with the bridesmaids clustered around the wedding arbor. Maybe someone was already tipsy? One of the bridesmaids ran to greet the new arrival and gave her a big hug. An obnoxious groomsman began catcalling and making exaggerated kissing noises. The bridesmaid turned to the groomsman and told him to shut the hell up. That was when I learned that "she" was the maid of honor's brother, Valerie.

She came over to the DJ table and asked me if there was assigned seating. I told her that anywhere was fine, except for the first row—parents of the bride and groom only. She sat down in the last row near my DJ table. Taking off her pumps, she began rubbing her feet. I made a comment about her shoes looking uncomfortable. She said I had no idea.

Yep. When you have all the wedding DJ and life experience I have, you can talk to anyone, about anything. Being able to communicate effectively with others has always been a strength of mine. I always know the perfect thing to say in any situation.

Valerie explained that she was starting her third month of living as a woman and had been on hormones that whole time. She also told me that the advice for transitioning was to dress modestly so as not to attract too much attention to early. A year before, she'd been asked by the bride to be one of the bridesmaids for the wedding. She declined. Valerie was nineteen and had known since age six that she was in the wrong body. I asked if there was anything she'd like to hear. Valerie requested some old-school Johnny Cash, "A Boy Named Sue."

The obnoxious groomsman came over wanting to know if I was going to play "good music." Most of his requests were already on the bride's playlist. He then pulled me aside, speaking loudly so Valerie could hear. He told me that Valerie was queer and used to be a man. I thanked him for his insight but added that it often takes one to know one. Valerie laughed. Brad left calling us a couple queers and giving me the finger.

I was expecting to find only BBQ and a sub-par potato salad in this country setting, maybe a drunken redneck or two, but not bravery. For a trans person to show up at this wedding with this crowd took balls. Valerie had a hell of a lot of guts and my respect.

August was just too damn hot.

September was just too damn busy.

October was just too damn weird.

I had four Halloween-themed weddings. Even one on the sacred night itself. On Halloween, I saw the return of the groundhog couple from February. They were now wearing enhanced costumes, embellished with real fur. Their tails looked a little bigger and pointier than I remembered.

The couple had requested that all guests dress in costume. And everybody did. The bride dressed as a bride, with her future husband dressed as a divorce lawyer. Nice. The bridesmaids coordinated their costumes to all be sexy witches. The groomsmen were all zombies. Go figure. I saw couples dressed as ketchup and mustard, Coke and Pepsi. One guest came looking like an insane version of Tesla. He ended up taking a very incorrigible Jane Austen back to his hotel room for some late-night champagne. So much for sense and sensibility. A family of six all dressed like the California Raisins.

I started to suspect that a guest's choice of costume had deeper meanings. Just like Glenda from the Lovey Dovey Lingerie Emporium could predict a couple's sexual proclivities based on her patented five-question quiz, I began to believe that a person's choice of Halloween costume also gave strong indications.

Those dressed as historical figures liked spontaneous sex, surprises, and numerous positions during coitus. Those dressing like condiments and food were into planned, destination-orientated romantic encounters. Also, these couples preferred only one or two sexual positions during coitus. The cartoon and nursery-rhyme people were somewhat spontaneous, but less adventuresome with other forms of sex play. Those dressing like rodents just liked it rough.

The World Trade Organization protest march took place in November 1999, just like the Artist Formerly Known As Prince had predicted. There wasn't any party, though, just a riot. My second son was a month old, and I was paying great attention to when and how often he passed his stool. The crusty end of his umbilical cord had finally fallen off, which helped with the frequent diapering. God, that kid had one hell of an innie. Besides, I was also busy working, you know, at a job, unlike most of the activists. I did catch some highlights on one of the local news stations. Nobody was really marching, just a lot of yelling. That made me sad.

When I was in junior high band, I loved marching down Main Street during the Daffodil Parade. While playing my alto clarinet, I'd swagger proudly wearing my cobalt-blue school blazer. On my right, in perfect stride with me, was the French (and very exotic) eighth-grader, Monique. In front, my Asian friend, Patrick. Julie Morgan at my rear. Leading the band, none other than the flamboyant Byron Jones. Boy, he really knew his way around a baton. My memories of marching with Monique and my friends brought me back to 1978 like a Hal Leonard arrangement of "Rubber Band Man" or "Walking in Rhythm."

Any group wanting to demonstrate or exercise free speech will always have my support, whether I agree or disagree with the message. That said, I expect that those protesting be orderly and respectful of others. Although protesters are generally angry to begin with, I think they should try to pull it together, like we all did during fire drills in second grade. Nice, orderly lines with our hands at our sides. I say, let your voice be heard, then go home. And be mindful of those sleep-deprived souls who've been diapering at odd hours. Maybe call the demonstration off a little early sometimes so everyone can go home and get some sleep.

I'm no genius, but I knew there'd be trouble when half the protesters showed up carrying gas masks. Most of what I saw on TV was a bunch of police standing on one side of a barrier and the protesters behind another. Someone started a car fire, which made a lot of smoke. The fire department had to put it out, so the police fired tear gas, which just made more smoke.

One highlight I saw, which was replayed over and over on the local news, involved the most radical of the protesters breaking windows in a Starbucks. After breaking the windows they stormed the establishment and trashed the place. It looked to be a group of five young men wearing masks. Giving them the benefit of the doubt, maybe they just really needed to use the restroom? Being more focused on correct diaper etiquette, I was merely bemused by the antics of the police and protesters.

After the tear gas cleared, most of the local government elites blamed the police for not dealing with the protesters effectively. This struck me as funny, since the person not having to negotiate a situation will often be the most critical of those who do. Those engaged in a crisis in real time simply don't have the luxury of hindsight or the comfort of tracking polling numbers for reelection before making a decision. I thought of the whole thing as being analogous to my newborn's latest stool. Nodding off while diapering, I dreamed a dreamy dream.

The protesters were coming. Only they weren't marching down 6th Avenue in Seattle. No. It was at the nearby Indian Casino, "The Number One Place for Fun," three miles from my house. The local agencies were meeting to discuss the pros and cons of privatizing diaper services. The radical idea was to provide greater choice (cloth or disposable) to the people within established delivery routes. The protesters were opposing the existence of diapers in any form. What next, a ban on plastic bags? Those damned socialists.

As it would happen, it was five in the afternoon before the anti-diaper activists were organized enough to begin their demonstration. After marching toward the casino they ran into a counter group—a hoard of locals heading to the casino to gamble after work and take advantage of the all-you-can-eat buffet. Both reached the main entrance at the same time. The anti-diaper crowd tried to stand their ground, but their leaders quickly, and wisely, yielded the right of way and devised a change of plan. The anti-diaper crowd would be no match for working Americans set on losing their weekly paychecks. It was also prime-rib night.

The anti-diaper dissidents reconciled that one should have the freedom to gamble with one's own money. Trust the public to decide the merits of cloth or disposable diapers? No way. The protesters left the casino and decided to march toward easier fair. Looking north, the dissidents figured that those diaper-loving patrons shopping for 40–60 percent off retail designer labels at the outlet mall would surely be easier targets. Oh, how little they knew.

Halfway between the casino and the outlet mall stood a Cabela's sporting-goods store. The protesters cheered. They all knew that Cabela's supported a person's right to keep and bear diapers. They'd break some windows, trash the place, use the restroom, grab a few bags of roasted pecans, maybe a double mocha? But this was a Cabela's, not a Starbucks.

When I think Starbucks, I think *nice*. Everyone there is always so friendly. In fact, you can sit there all day hogging the Wi-Fi, and nobody will say anything to you, except nice things. They're just really nice people.

When I think about Cabela's, I think about concealed-carry permits and armed, middle-aged women. At a Cabela's, you have less Wi-Fi but more sex appeal and firepower. You also have mothers with young children who don't have the luxury of idling about all day on free Wi-Fi, like some metrosexual version of Rip Van Winkle. These mothers and proud gun owners are busy taking care of their children and have already made sacrifices and the tough choices. Believe me, nobody wants to mess around with a mother of four pushing a stroller and packing a 9mm.

Sensing danger, the loving mothers escorted their children to the rear of the store. Being prepared for any eventuality, the mothers placed hearing protection on their children, prior to switching off their firearms' safeties. Those women with prior military experience exited the side of the building to later coordinate a flanking move with the matriarchal store manager on headset. A hundred women would stand against the tens of thousands. They'd meet and greet the devils at the door.

The matriarchal militia chose to ignore the first feckless barrage of unscented baby wipes thrown but would provide a double dose of hell's fury following the next. The second round, scented wipes this time, were thrown by the protesters. The middle-aged, muffin-topped, militia fired their guns. But they weren't shooting bullets. Out the ends of their guns came the dirty diapers of every child they'd ever changed. They were hideous projectiles, most overflowing with what had once been puréed peas or rice cereal mixed with breast milk. Many of the looters went down in the first volley as the wettest diapers, hit them like bags of wet cement.

The remaining protesters were outflanked by the classic pincer move used at the Battle of the Bulge during WWII and were pinned down by veterans behind minivans throwing Venti double-mocha grenades. The women quickly carried the day.

After defiling the dead, the mothers garnered their children, and everybody went out for makeovers. Then it was off to the all-you-can-eat buffet. If you're a wuss, loot a Starbucks. If you want to be a real anarchist, try a Cabela's.

The final wedding of 1999 was on New Year's Eve. The reception hall was right on the ocean. And sometimes it was in the ocean as well. Forget about global warming for a minute. The idiots just built the thing too close to the beach. In the '90s people would do anything for a water view. The area experienced extremely high tides about twice a year. During the week leading up, there'd been a new moon, with Jupiter, the sun, and even Uranus pulling and pushing during high tide.

The mega tide had flooded the wedding venue and parking lot before receding, leaving acres of dead and dying starfish and several spawning salmon high and dry. The starfish didn't have a chance, with most freezing to death the following night. The survival-minded salmon were making the best of it in the runoff pond next to the handicapped parking.

None of the bridal party or guests were willing to park in the lot closest to the hall. Decaying starfish, by nature, are slippery and prone to smelling badly. No moral qualms here. Driving into the lower lot, I enjoyed the slush, slush, slush, followed by the occasional crunch. It made me nostalgic for crab season.

At the couple's request, the groomsmen rerouted the guests to an overflow parking lot uphill. This lot was flooded with the years' accumulation of condoms and hypodermic needles. I'll stick with the rotting starfish and horny salmon any day.

The plan was to start the ceremony at 3:00 PM. The briny hall was roughly the size of a gymnasium. Due to the recent flooding, the only working electrical outlet in the entire venue was in the ladies' restroom. So, I had to run three hundred feet of extension cord to set up for the ceremony. The bridal party arrived hours before for pictures, with the early guests hitting the open bar.

Preceremony music had been playing for over an hour before the bridal party was lined up and ready to begin. Finally. I hit the music, track one. Nobody moved. I turned up the volume and nodded toward the bridal party to start. Still, nobody moved. Checking the date on my DJ file, I noticed that the agenda and music I was using was from a wedding the month before. The guests ware getting impatient. So, in a moment of panic, I played the next selection. Magically, they started to march. It was Whitney Houston singing "It's Not Right, But It's Okay." I had no clue if this was even close to the music I was supposed to be playing.

Next up, the couple. I faded to the next selection on the disc. "Smooth" by Santana. The couple just smiled and marched down the aisle toward the minister. Being on a roll, I played the subsequent selection from the same disc for their recessional. It was "Livin' la Vida Loca" by Ricky Martin. After hearing the recessional music start, the couple smiled at me before showing me their middle fingers and walking out. I cut to selection five on the disc. It was "Two Out of Three Ain't Bad" by Meatloaf.

At the reception, the caterers were sucking the power out of the speakers. Every time the hotplates cycled through, the subwoofer lights dimmed, and I had to drop the volume to keep from tripping the breaker. I played "1999" by Prince about twenty times, as well as a bunch of standard wedding fare. Eventually I found the couple's one-of-a-kind wedding-day agenda and got the rest of their reception events correct. The celebration peaked by nine thirty. By ten thirty there was no food or drink. Just the occasional rotting starfish going squish on the dance floor. Most of the guests were gone by eleven, following the couple's example.

There was no longer a party. Only ten lost souls remained waiting to bring in the new year. The caterers and their hot plates had all gone home, so I could bump the music to a moderate volume if I could do nothing else.

The half hour between eleven thirty and midnight was the longest two hours of my life. One of the groomsmen volunteered to do the countdown to welcome in the new year but screwed it up because he was unable to read his watch correctly. A bridesmaid caught it more or less in time. but we all welcomed in the new year a few minutes late. Happy New Year? Y2K? Whoop-de-fuckin'-doo! After a few minutes of celebration the crowd went outside to smoke and wave sparklers on the beach. The couple had paid me to play till one thirty, and that's what the bride's sister wanted me do. After playing to an empty room for over an hour, I shut everything down.

Loading out, I ran into some of the locals. They were trying their waterfront version of the DJ Hustle. The hustle? Street people start to show up when the DJ's loading out. They offer to help for some cash. They assure you that none of your stuff will get stolen or broken, so long as they're around. I'd tap danced this tango before. I took my CD cases back inside and called 911. A patrol car was already in the area, big surprise.

Before leaving, the disgruntled locals felt the need to empty their bladders and what remained of their forty-ounce malt liquors onto my car. After the police arrived, I came out and thanked the officer. She said she'd stay if I wanted. No need. Pulling away the officer got a good look at the rear plate of my Ford Focus. Shit, she saw the expired tabs. This month it had come down to a second crib and diapers or car tabs. I was two months delinquent. So the officer wrote me a ticket.

While loading out equipment, I became startled by the passionate throes of mating salmon. Slipping on one of the decomposing semifrosted starfish, a 120-pound speaker fell on my foot. My big toe broke, followed by the speaker breaking in half. The pieces slid down the slippery sidewalk into the runoff pond, scaring the hell out of the salmon. Seizing, drooling, and inarticulate swearing followed. Hobbling on one foot, I finished loading up the car, hopping and hoping the locals wouldn't return. Backing out of the parking spot, I ran over a malt-liquor bottle left under my tire. I prayed that I wouldn't get a flat before reaching home.

I entered the new year with a compound fracture of the big toe and two halves of a thousand-dollar speaker left floating in a runoff pond. Both rear tires were flat by morning. Replacing the speaker, new tires, doctor visit, and ticket for expired tabs, would cost me over three thousand dollars. The wedding paid six hundred.

The following day, I began to think about the bridal show later in January. A chance to do it all over again. For it was now the year 2000. But more importantly, we were all still here. I guess the Artist Formerly Known As Prince got it wrong.

BLINKING IN A SNOWSTORM

S ITTING IN AN uncomfortable theater chair, I was exposed to the musical production of *Avenue Q*, a lyrical, funny, perverse romp involving puppets, people, a porn-addicted cookie monster, and, of course, Gary Coleman—but not the real "Whatchu talkin' 'bout, Willis?" Gary Coleman from *Diff'rent Strokes*. The musical, created by Robert Lopez, Jeff Marx, and Jeff Whitty involved X-rated puppet sex, and, yes, Gary Coleman singing that Broadway favorite "Everyone's a Little Bit Racist." The adult Gary in this production was portrayed by a black woman in her mid-thirties.

Having grown up in the whitest vestibules in the 1960s, I quickly learned that the concept of whiteness was only an idealization. I was surrounded by so much whiteness that one need only envision the perpetual winter in the first book of Narnia or a glacier encompassing North America a hundred thousand years ago with hints of brilliant blue for the eyes.

When I say I'm white I don't mean white like the lumpy snow of mid-January; I'm quite pink. Light-pink or pale-beige would describe my entire family and most of the neighborhood.

When I think back, I also reminisce fondly about the finger-sized crayons in my boyhood seven-piece coloring kit. This was a 1960s standard-issue necessity for those beginning pedagogy and my first encounter with the concepts of other colors. I might mention that this same kit also came with a complimentary pocketknife. Yes, my preschool coloring set contained seven friendly crayons and a knife, which if brought to school today would get you expelled and put on a terrorist watch list.

While examining my crayon kit on the first day of kindergarten I remember our teacher, Mrs. Harris, having us take crayons out of the box, one at a time, so she could clearly state each color. We replied in a call-and-response routine, holding up the corresponding crayon in a Stalinistic salute.

Some of my fellow classmates were too impulsive to follow these directions. Others would simply dump their crayons and knife on the table helter-skelter, exploring the whole kit as one great gestalt. This, of course, could not be tolerated. After all, we were in kindergarten now and attending an almost exclusively white school in the suburbs during the 1960s. We had standards.

A few of the students who were unable to desist from their aberrant crayon behavior were later placed in special classes. A red-headed boy named Charles sat at my table. Charles had difficulty selecting the correct crayon color when asked to do so. I'd help him by picking up my own crayon first, hoping he'd learn through my example.

Charles became frustrated when corrected about his crayon choice. He was moved to his own table after recess. There he sat, alone. By the end of our first day, Charles was refusing to pick up any crayons at all. When encouraged by Mrs. Harris to pick up his orange crayon, Charles put his hands over his ears.

That was on a Tuesday. Charles was a no-show for Wednesday and Thursday. His name tag was removed from his chair and table space on Friday. Just like that, Charles was gone. Afterward, when Mrs. Harris told us to pick up our orange crayons, we did.

I never saw Charles during the rest of my public-school experience, though he did manage a debut comeback on *America's Most Wanted* in 1989. His was a short, three-minute story with an unpleasant ending.

Back to weapons in school... my entire kindergarten class had the same coloring kit, containing seven crayons and a knife. I guess the knife was included to sharpen the crayons? Hello? Or possibly to provide a last line of defense against communist Russia should they invade. This was the height of the Cold War, and no commie was going to take our freedom or our crayons. The knife resembled a little Swiss Army knife about an inch long. And sharp.

On one occasion, my best friend, Byron Jones, sharpened his green crayon to resemble what my mom would call a man's pee pee before accidently dropping his knife. As an adult, I've clumsily mishandled cutlery countless times, only to have it bounce off my slacks and tumble harmlessly to the floor.

But this knife was a sharp, little bastard. It cut straight through Byron's plaid bell-bottom pants. We're talking heavy polyester. Byron screamed. And the blood? Let me tell you, everybody had red crayons that day.

Our beloved Mrs. Harris came rushing over. Gazing at the horror, she screamed, then noticed the exquisite detailing of Byron's crayon. She stood transfixed, as though suddenly remembering some long-lost love, daydreamingly oblivious that one of her students was bleeding out. A second round of screams shook her from her reverie, and she called the main office. She pocketed the crayon.

The elderly school nurse, Ms. Tracy, waddled down to the kindergarten wing and successfully removed Byron from the class in a WWII-issue wheelchair. His screams were no match for the screeching of the rusted wheels and bearings. Either Byron or the wheelchair gave a final screech, and the class was back to unabashed crayon exploration once again, minus one student and one very special green crayon.

Nurse Tracy successfully removed both the knife and what remained of Byron's pants. She was able to stop the bleeding. The knife was removed from all our kits following a second bloody tragedy a month later.

When I was in the second grade, I heard a rumor that Nurse Tracy kept a bottle of vodka in her desk. This, of course, we'll never know because Nurse Tracy died in a car accident two years later, following a staff Christmas party. According to the police report her car was seen leaving the road "at a high rate of speed."

I ran into Byron during the '90s at an art happening in a warehouse loft downtown. He was well-dressed, drinking a cosmopolitan, and smoking clove cigarettes. Byron was a sculptor, and judging by the samples on display, still inspired by the green crayon that he'd crafted in kindergarten. If Mrs. Harris had been there, she'd have been so proud.

I neglected to bring up the knife incident out of fear of

embarrassing him. But judging by his artistic vision, that singular event had had a profound influence on his work. I was poorly dressed, smoking Camel Lights, and invisible to the huge personalities of most of the attendees.

From the first time I could hold a crayon in my pasty pink hand, it was obvious how distinct color was on white paper. No denying it. Attending almost exclusively white schools growing up, any minority student stuck out—yes, like color on white paper. Conversely, the white crayon shone most brightly on black paper, like the white eyes I drew on my black construction-paper bat for Halloween.

In seventh grade I became friends with Patrick. He was Japanese and sat next to me in band playing the tenor saxophone. I played alto clarinet. This was my first friendship with a real Asian dude. Prior, I'd only had a pretend TV Asian friend: George Takei from *Star Trek*. I always enjoyed his Sulu character on reruns I watched as a child. That look he gave the camera while firing phasers or locking on photon torpedoes? Shivers. He was also very good about keeping the deflector shields up.

During the rest of his time on the bridge, Sulu sported a pleasant but concerned smile. Considering he had to share the sound stage for three seasons with Bill Shatner, Mr. Takei may be a better actor than any of us will ever know.

Patrick's grandparents owned a small grocery store in the valley near our junior high. Patrick and I would leave school grounds after football practice to get free soda. His grandmother occasionally commented that I looked like Andy Gibb of the Bee Gees. I didn't think I looked like Andy Gibb all that much, but free soda was free soda.

I do remember the song "Shadow Dancing," though, and doing the bump for the first time during the junior high dance with an eighth-grader named Monique. She was French. Our first dance as a couple of diversity turned out badly. We performed more of a "hump" than a "bump." In the middle of our dance, Monique was asked to leave the cafeteria by the vice principal because she appeared to be the one instigating the thrusting in what he described as our "perverted, overly sexualized, flesh festival of immorality." And in front of seventh-graders, no less! I went outside to console her. We held each other's sweaty hands until her dad came to pick her up.

Patrick's grandparents were robbed a few years later. The incident made the local news. His grandmother described the perpetrators as two white guys under twenty-five who looked like Andy Gibb. I was sorry for her family's loss of over three hundred dollars but wasn't optimistic that the robbers would ever be apprehended. In 1979, two Andy Gibbs stepping into my community would disappear like polar bears blinking in a snowstorm.

I went to see Cheap Trick in 1980. At fifteen, you couldn't call yourself a man unless you skipped school, bought a rock jersey of the band you were seeing, and smoked marijuana within city limits. On top of all that, if you could manage to make out with a big-haired girl during the concert, you were a legend.

My friend Frank and I arrived late due to traffic. We weren't concerned about getting good seats since we were planning to stand on the floor in front of the stage. We'd mosh our path to the stage, get high, and when the concert was over we'd leave as men. We wanted to be as close as possible to the most stylishly dressed guitar player in the world, Rick Nielsen. I loved him in tweeds.

Despite being frisked from head to toe, I managed to conceal a small pipe in my navel and a baggie of weed in my underpants. Inside the arena the smell of marijuana was overpowering, as was the number of young people. But the concert hall was also full of diversity. Asian people, black people, brown people, yellow people. My entire crayon box in one place at the same time.

My fellow crayons and I began smoking pot together. After sharing several bowls of my homegrown, I did indeed "Surrender" to the love and joy of my newfound friends. Soon mama was all right, daddy was all right, Asians were all right, black guys, the handicapped, we were all all right, we just seemed a little weird. After my third bowl, I met the "Dream Police."

I never hooked up with a big-haired girl, but I did manage to put a cute young lady named Niko on my shoulders during "I Want You to Want Me." I think she liked me, but she may have just wanted to see the band for at least a few minutes during the evening instead of a bunch of shoulder blades. I set her down and watched her four-foot-seven-inch frame disappear into the crowd. My new black friend wearing sunglasses shook his head and mouthed the word "Nice."

While working in the primarily Hispanic school districts of the lower valley, I was exposed as a member of the great-white minority. I was no longer a polar bear blinking in a snowstorm but a lone, white crayon on a brown piece of construction paper the size of Rhode Island.

At the elementary level, some of the Hispanic boys called me MacGyver and threw quips my way, such as,

"How are you going to escape this week?" and "Where's your Jeep?" I was blond, lean, and rangy, sporting a modified mullet and did bear a slight resemblance to MacGyver, circa 1985-1992, portrayed by Richard Dean Anderson. At first, I thought the moniker was endearing.

However, during my second year at the school a new janitor was hired, and he was also referred to as MacGyver by the students. He was a balding, overweight, white guy of sixty-five who came out of retirement to save his hop farm. Apparently white guys in 1990 all looked like MacGyver through the eyes of migrant children.

On a singular day, I met with a new family from Central America, and during the winter months my skin would get so white... how white was it? Upon seeing me, three of the younger children ran behind their parents screaming, "Monstruo yeti muy blanco!" The parents spoke quietly to the children, reassuring them that they had no reason to fear the albino and that the real yeti lived in the Himalayas far, far away.

Yes, if I got a peso for every time a lower-valley resident gestured in my direction during the month of February, I could've bought a taco truck. The phrase "muy blanco" was actually my first introduction to Spanish. Reflecting, I think many of my Latino brethren just thought I was in ill health. They weren't staring so much as deciding whether or not to call an ambulance before I collapsed from chronic anemia.

I was DJing a wedding in 2005 at a four-star hotel downtown. I met with the couple prior, per the usual routine, to plan the event. On the day of the wedding, I learned that the brides' brother Jayden would be doing some of the announcements. The family was from Jamaica and very rich.

The ceremony had been performed outdoors in the hotel garden by a minister from the Universalist Church. The reception that followed was to be held in the most spacious ballroom of the upper-end hotel whose name I refuse to mention. Take away my DJ-reserved parking spot the day of the wedding and you'll get no free press from me, bastards.

The bride's brother was pretentious and preening. Jayden was short. His announcements during the reception were long and pointless meanderings, pleading embarrassments for attention. The attempts at humor, lame.

After the dancing had begun I was approached by Jayden and several of his friends. He had come to pay off the balance of my fee. Great. I showed him the invoice, and he began fanning what must have been five thousand dollars or so in hundred-dollar bills. If the bride and groom wanted to buy more time, I'd be willing to play my entire music library until the following Thursday if they were up for it.

But then Jayden began a weird gyrating type of fan dance. He'd slowly wave the money in my face and quickly pull it back. He started smiling while waving his left index finger in a no, no sort of gesture. Was this a traditional dance for the DJ?

His friends stood behind him waiting to see what I was going to do. The money dance continued. After several moments, I was tempted to hold up one particular finger as well but decided that a slow fade to Usher's "Yeah" was a better choice.

Fade completed, I pointed to the $250 balance

printed clearly at the bottom of the invoice. Jayden danced. It was obvious he had the cash. After laying down a single hundred-dollar bill on top of my CD changer, he asked if it was enough? Pausing, he then laid the second Franklin down, inquiring again, "Enough?" Since most things come in threes, he began to lay down the third, then took it away. I told him I could make change on his hundred if he wanted to settle. His friends moved closer to the DJ table and began setting their pint-sized microbrews on my playlists and CDs, crowding me and my equipment.

Not getting the response he wanted, Jayden picked up the Franklin twins and said that he didn't think I was doing a very good job. He wasn't going to pay me anything. He and his friends left, leaving their microbrews dripping on my equipment.

Fifteen minutes later, Jayden came back on his own palming a fresh beer, no dancing. He threw five Franklins in my face without saying a word. Two of the bills landed on the DJ table, and three fell to the floor. I waited until he left before I knelt to pick up the money. The rest of the wedding was uneventful. At the end of the night I drove home. The couple sent me a thank-you note two weeks later telling me I was the best wedding DJ they'd ever seen.

According to Gary Coleman and the puppets, we're all a little bit racist. Minus the knife, my crayon box is a very peaceful place of color.

THE BRIDE, THE GROOM, AND THE WARDROBE

AT THE CENTER of the Chronicles of Narnia is a battle between good and evil. Also a talking lion that doesn't wear pants. Mr. Tumnus also doesn't wear pants, and he's an animal below the waist. Say what?! There are four adorable kids who are encouraged by a weird unmarried uncle to explore a wardrobe, which is a lot like a closet. So, the premise of these children's books is that children should be closeted and have imaginary adventures until they're forced out by a pantless lion.

There's a white witch who freezes everybody, and there are references to free will and mankind's need to make its own choices to, say, not wear pants. But the real reason the children must leave Narnia is because they grow up. They're forced to put aside childish things and become adults. This includes accepting the trappings of a job, money, and marriage.

If I know anything, it's that little has changed in my fifty-plus years regarding your standard wedding. Oh, of course nobody's singing "Evergreen" or "We've Only Just Begun" during the ceremony anymore like they did in the 1970s. Thank God. I remember being six and sweating profusely while being regaled by the musical adaptation of the Lord's Prayer. Being chubby didn't help. You sweat more when you're chubby. Like everyone else, including Uncle David, the caterers, and the members of the bridal party, I was wearing uncomfortable clothes.

Today, now that marriage is legal for everyone, you may have two grooms traipsing down the aisle, the wedding dress optional. Or maybe two brides with one wearing a rented tux. I've seen and done it all.

However, the majority of the weddings I've DJ'd were boy meets girl, boy proposes to girl, or girl proposes to boy (you'd be surprised). The bride and groom exchange vows, forever committing themselves to the only person they'll ever love. Blah, blah, blah.

Okay, now for the elephant in the room. The bride. The wedding is all about the bride. I'm trying to be sexist here. The bride gets a wedding dress for five thousand dollars and wears it once; the groom gets a rented tux with God knows how many dry-cleaned sweat stains. The bride's ring has the largest diamond the couple cannot afford; the groom sports a plain band.

After the wedding, the dress is vacuum sealed, put away, and cherished for years to come; the groom gets charged a fee for returning his tux a day late and a dry-cleaning bill for spilling rigatoni on the lapel at the reception.

The groomsmen fair no better. They also sport rented fashions, beer-stained from performing keg stands at last week's wedding. Occasionally the bridesmaids are expected to buy their own dresses, but most often they're provided, courtesy of the family. Sadly, these dresses are seldom worn again. The vast majority of them seem to end up being reprocessed into community-theater costumes for musical adaptations of *Mamma Mia*.

Throughout the 1970s, as women made their way toward equality, there were many bra burnings. I know because I attended every one of them, hoping to lend support. Whether young or old, gay or straight., all women have at least thought about their wedding day. Most do not want to accept this premise, but I can assure you that it's absolutely true. Even if the bride has never thought of herself as a girly girl, she will eventually entertain at least passing thoughts about the special day. She may experience matrimonial reverie while driving her tractor or hunting an elk, but make no mistake, the vision will come. Her ideas might be lousy, but ideas she will have.

Unfortunately, the mother of the bride will have ideas too, and so will family and friends, married or not. The already married will try to relive their wedding experience vicariously. Many will wish to embellish. The mother of the bride was lucky to convince the church to allow her to marry before the baby bump showed, and any addition to her shotgun-wedding memories is greatly appreciated.

The matron of honor didn't have a chocolate fountain with strawberries, but her new sister-in-law sure as heck will. The bride's unmarried friends usually resort to being "yes women" who agree eagerly with the bride about everything. After all, they're not the ones paying.

Installing a chocolate fountain, planting a tree, releasing butterflies and pigeons, mixing sand, lighting candles, dance teams, bouncy houses, harpists, or barber-shop quartets, these matrimonial accessories can quickly become psychological trappings that derange the mind.

Champagne fountains, hot-air-balloon rides, personal labels on water or wine bottles, photo booths, skydivers, fire-breathers, flash mobs, where does it end?

I've witnessed several magicians capable of making a couple's money disappear. The card tricks are always a welcome distraction while waiting for the buffet. During the cake cutting, one of them gave the bride a magic wand that exploded into a floral bouquet to the applause of the guests. After the magician got his tip he performed his final illusion and disappeared.

I've seen real clowns (not drunk groomsmen) with red noses, white makeup, suspenders, and big shoes. All the clowns I worked with were dedicated professionals. But seeing a clown terrifies me. When I think *clown*, I think *circus* and can't help envisioning Dumbo's mother in the original 1941 version, chained up in her pen, reaching out to her floppy-eared son with her trunk. Spoiler alert, the baby's taken from her in one hell of a tearjerker. Walt Disney forever ruined the whole circus experience for me. Even a carnival elicits anxiety.

I saw *Pinocchio* as part of the same Disney double feature. The scene where the cigar-smoking boys are turned into jackasses scarred me for life. And after seeing the raft scene, where the giant whale tries to kill Pinocchio and Geppetto, I spent years being afraid of goldfish. Mr. Disney, my shrink and the antidepressant manufacturers thank you.

Back to clowns. I think adult wedding guests tire too quickly of balloon animals to justify a professional clown. I did see a real clown drunk at a wine tasting once. Not funny. Not funny at all. The only thing I haven't seen at a wedding is someone selling term life-insurance policies between the best man's toast and the couple's first dance, but I know it's only a matter of time.

And then came *Mamma Mia*. That damned movie caused bridal psychosis on a level seldom seen outside reality shows, such as *Say Yes to the Dress* or *Bridezillas*. During the wedding season following *Mamma Mia*'s debut, every bride was envisioning flash mobs of their sisters and bridal-party members all dancing down to a yacht on the Mediterranean to the tune of "Dancing Queen." I can play all the ABBA you want at the reception, but there will be no professionally choreographed dance routines. These are your family members, not a Vegas floor show. And there's simply no way to transform a 150-year-old warehouse into a small Greek island. I'm good, but not *that* good. Brides want their weddings to be unique, but they all watch the same movies.

The groom. You may have met your future bride when she was a pigtailed cutie in your kindergarten class. Perhaps you looked up while coloring to see her sitting next to your best friend, Byron Jones. You were shy but mustered up the courage of a nine-year-old and asked to borrow her green crayon. She smiled toothlessly and lisped a whistling, "Yeths." So it begins.

Maybe you met your French beauty at the junior high dance. You tripped the light fantastic to Andy Gibb's "Shadow Dancing" where the two of you successfully performed the bump in front of all the seventh-graders. After leaving the cafeteria you held hands.

Others met through happenstance. In 1980, at the Cheap Trick concert, your big-haired date stood you up. Heartbroken, you resigned yourself to smoking homegrown in front of the stage while admiring Rick Nielsen in tweeds. Even though you were surrounded by your new friends of diversity, you remained wanting and lonely.

You turned, as if kissed by a rainbow, and there she was, standing behind you the whole time, looking at your shoulder blades. You placed her petite, four-foot-seven frame high upon the pedestal of your manly shoulders and sang together "Surrender."

It's never a matter of if, for the groom, the question is always when. You'll meet The One, and when you do, your toes curl, your palms sweat. This is soon followed by long phone calls, dating, third base, the fights, coitus, breaking up, coitus, making up, coitus. Years later, you agree to secure your union by attending a bridal show. You thought it was called a wedding expo, but you go because you love her. While airing down row C you remember tasting a cake sample and learning about colonics. A satisfied grin crosses your face when you think back to the Lovey Dovey Lingerie Emporium's booth. You remember how you were lovingly slapped by your future bride for fondling one of the large-breasted mannequins. Later in the day, you win a free vibrator.

So, today, on your wedding day, you look out to see the insurance agent who sold you term life. Seated next to him is a very serious-looking man, probably a stationer. The music begins, and you are brought full circle as you see the lovable, geriatric, tired-looking DJ. He returns your gaze with a comforting bus-driver nod that you once thought signaled a three-way. Welcome aboard, the DJ says with a toothy smirk. Your bride enters in white, holding her bouquet.

Overwhelmed with joy, you gently tap an old but

cherished green crayon hidden in the breast pocket of the rented tux. You truly love your new wife.

But what if the groom was the one planning this wedding? If so, it would consist of a ceremony no longer than three minutes with no tuxes. At the reception there would be lots of BBQ, paper plates, some of that delicious potato salad from the deli that comes in plastic containers and, of course, beer. Instead of a wedding cake there'd be twinkies or donuts, purchased by the best man at the gas station on the day of the reception. Just kidding. Most grooms go along with and enjoy the more extravagant wedding festivities, like releasing butterflies or dipping strawberries in the chocolate fountain. Indeed, by the day of the wedding most resolve to just send in the clowns.

The pink elephant in the room waiting to crush the groom is drinking too much at the reception. My experience? Grooms who drink regularly are rarely an issue. If twenty-five-year-old Fred is used to downing three cold ones several times a week, I'm not worried about him tipping four or five during the reception. An experienced drinker also knows to skip the sweet, cheap champagne from the bacteria-laden fountain.

But the teetotaling groom is the last person you want drinking anywhere. He has no experience or tolerance and usually ends up puking or crying or both. Nondrinkers who cut loose at the wedding tend to drink badly. All the grooms I've witnessed being hoisted horizontally into the limo at the end of the night were inexperienced drinkers.

The guests demonstrate similar drinking profiles. Within an hour of any reception, I can pick out those who'll make it and those who won't. I feel like a battle-hardened lieutenant looking over a new batch of troops and knowing in short order who's going to make it home and who isn't, at least not standing up.

The wardrobe. There's even special bridal underwear for the special day. I know because I've seen it. I've often been summoned by the bride just prior to the ceremony to discuss last-minute changes. I'm shown into her sacred bridal dressing chamber, and there she stands in her smalls or sometimes not-so-smalls. Often the bridesmaids are also in stages of undress.

I remember seeing women's underwear ads in magazines from the 1960s and '70s. The ads showed five or six women just standing or sitting around in their underwear talking. Sure, it was just an underwear ad, but I've noticed that women tend to have greater solidarity for that kind of thing.

As a wedding DJ you have the nonjudgmental ear of a bartender and, since you see people in their underwear, you have the access of a masseuse. A partially dressed bridal party will divulge all sorts of family secrets and opinions to the DJ without prejudice, for you have no family affiliation. They assume you're willing to listen to any concern regarding their wedding, life choices, or even doubts about the groom. My professional ethics as a DJ kept me from staring at people in their underwear, but hey, everybody looks.

Not all brides are dressed in the sexy, honeymoon-night lingerie you see in the catalogs or on cable. Seldom did I view the regal lingerie corset from Victoria's Secret. Most brides wear whatever torturous body-shaping device is required to get the dress to fit. Behind the scenes, there's a lot of painful tucking, pinning, and pulling. Once I went back to get a clarification on how the bride wanted her parents introduced, only to witness the bride's mother taping her daughter's breasts. I didn't know you could do that.

On one occasion, everyone was standing around in their underwear, including the bride, groom, groomsmen, the father of the bride, and the ring bearer. They were huddled around the only air conditioner in the entire church trying to keep from passing out in the 105-degree August heat. At another wedding the bride saved me the trip and walked out to discuss last-minute irregularities with myself and the photographer; she was wearing only breast petals, which act a lot like tape, and a thong. I don't know if the groom got to see his bride before the wedding, but the entire catering staff sure did.

Conventional wisdom says it's bad luck for the groom to see the bride before the wedding. However, half the couples I've worked with were living together prior to marriage. You may have seen your future wife in half the positions of the Kama Sutra, but God forbid you see her taped breasts the day of the wedding.

For the groom, it's the rented tux. The cummerbund, tails, and top hat are optional. As far as undergarments for the wedding? I think the average groom spends all of about two seconds deciding whether it's boxers or briefs on the day of the wedding, if it crosses his mind at all.

For one memorable wedding, the bride's grandmother insisted on sewing the bridesmaids' dresses. Her choice was a halter-style dress with a fruit-patterned theme. I started the processional music, and out came the cute, little flower girl with a cherry-print dress. Following was the younger sister of the bride in her plum-print dress. Next, the bride's bestie from college with two oranges strategically placed on the bodice. Then came the pineapple express—yep, one pineapple on each side of her dress the size of a cocktail napkin. Was nobody seeing this but me? Finally, out came the watermelons on the matron of honor, covering each breast. The bridesmaid's processional had been arranged by cup size. That's one creative fashion statement, grandma. They looked fabulous, though, standing together like a big fruit salad ready to be tossed.

The wedding had been delayed twenty minutes. I was replaying the preceremony music when I was asked to go and check on the bride. She was clothed but crying. The delay in the ceremony was due to the zipper of her five thousand-dollar, corset-style wedding dress. The zipper was fine, but the stitching had ripped. Her mother relayed to me, quite factually, that "The dress was made to fit tightly to give my Nancy some lift through the bodice." Yep. They were trying to use pins. I told the bride's mother that I'd bought my wife some breast tape and would be willing to share. She declined. All appeared lost.

But seated in the second row wearing a brown hat sat Aunty June, a sturdy woman of seventy-nine. She arose from her chair, sensing that something was wrong. Being clairvoyant, she picked up her purse and made her way toward the bride. This formidable seamstress knew at a glance the problem and solution. Aunty June pulled out her sewing kit and began sewing the bride into her dress with a basting stitch. The needle in her hand was a blur of dexterity, precision, and artistry. In less than two minutes the bride was sewn securely into her dress for the duration of the evening. After taking her father's arm, the bride marched down the aisle and was relinquished to her handsome groom. No one was the wiser, except the bride, her mother, Aunty June, and the DJ. As the bride and groom were getting ready to leave on their honeymoon, Aunty June gave the groom her antique ivory seam ripper as a memento. He would be the one to free his bride before their night of endless love. It was so romantic I teared up.

One bride, I fear, may have seen one too many episodes of *Masterpiece Theatre*. Her dress was so large and heavy that she had to wear a "cage" to support the yards of bridal satin, brocade, and tulle. I saw her in her cage before the wedding. The thing was made of thick steel cables and wiring. It looked heavy and damned uncomfortable. Talk about crimes of fashion.

Out stepped the groom and minister. I started the music for the bridal party. "Evergreen," a great choice. Five groomsmen with their maids and matrons of honor began the procession. What a gorgeous group. Now, it was the bride's moment. I started her musical selection, one of my favorites, and out she came. She was truly breathtaking, resembling an ivory Cinderella with her cathedral train blowing in the afternoon breeze. The bride was a rather petite five foot five with a dress twice as wide as she was tall. Her father reached to take her hand the way a person stretches when hanging out of a car window to open a mailbox they parked too far away from. He didn't wish to tread on her beautiful dress.

They started forward on cue, just like the rehearsal dinner the night before. The guests rose and turned to see the glorious spectacle. She was a princess. In her dress, she appeared to float toward the guests and family on the wings of angels. All present gasped at her beauty. She'd obviously chosen the right dress. But what was also becoming obvious was that her eight-foot-wide dress would not fit between the two-and-a-half-foot-wide aisle set up by the catering staff.

After reaching the first row of chairs she became a parade float. The empty chairs began toppling as though bowing in patronage. The chairs in the second row, however, were occupied, as were those in the third, and so on. Chairs and guests were being mowed down by her bridal crest. Guests were diving right and left to avoid being swallowed up by the tsunami of white tulle. Her bridal train crashed like a rogue wave, dragging the innocent out to sea behind her. Oh, the humanity! Undaunted, the bride continued. Her father now ran ahead to clear her way of chairs and patrons. It was chaos. He cleared chairs with guests still in them, sometimes two at a time, in a Herculean effort. Some simply lay where they'd fallen to wallow in her bridal trough.

Onward she came. She was her father's daughter. She'd wear her dress and marry that son of a bitch waiting for her at the altar. She arrived as "We've Only Just Begun" came to its climax. I started the applause, which was brought up in refrain by the guests and family. The applause for her "Charge of the White Brocade," as it came to be known, lasted for several minutes. A few moments later, they were husband and wife.

A wedding, much like Narnia, is a fantasy. Marriage really does come down to two people wearing uncomfortable clothes and saying, "I do."

FOLIE À DEUX

LAYING CONSCIOUS ON a gurney during my colonoscopy, I had a vision. After all, there's nothing like Magellan and Captain Hook circumnavigating all six feet of your large colon to make one introspective. From the moment the good doctor passed the point of no return and instructed the nurse to assist him in pushing the scope over my right hepatic flexures, I knew. Or, maybe it was the near puncturing of my right lung that brought everything into crystalline focus. People are delusional.

Staying conscious for the procedure was a bit vain, I admit. Of course, anyone wanting to see if the inside of their ass was as attractive as the outside probably has narcissistic tendencies to begin with. I've been told I have a dancer's butt, you see. Modesty aside, though, I've always had a "gut feeling" that I have a tapeworm. When younger, I figured my stomachaches were due to eating too many leaded paint chips and drinking contaminated tap water. Only later did I realize that intestinal distress could be a clear sign of something more serious. Tapeworms. Intestinal parasites by their nature have a great appetite for B vitamins, specifically B12, which would account for my lighter-shade-of-pale skin tone.

I was hoping, in a fatalistic sort of way, that we'd run

into Mr. Tapeworm so my suspicions would be confirmed. I really have no idea what happens when a gastroenterologist runs into a tapeworm. But I envisioned an epic life-and-death encounter, similar to a sperm whale and giant squid exchanging death throws a mile beneath the ocean. A vicious first attack by Mr. Tapeworm, followed by a counterattack of twenty-first-century weaponry.

After several minutes, the parasite would succumb to the suffocating vacuum clamp. The coup de grâce? The worm's death by laser, vanquished like a harmless intestinal polyp. After the battle, what remained of the carcass would be brought to the surface to be later mounted in my den. Oh, the stories I could tell the grandkids.

While taking this fantastic voyage, if you will, I was also curious to see if I ever passed that dime I swallowed as a five-year-old. After swallowing it, I looked in the toilet every day for almost a week. Ten cents was twice my weekly allowance in 1968. Mr. Roosevelt never left the White House as far as I could tell.

On the video monitor I was hoping to see our 32ND president mounted on the side of my large intestine, like a miniature variation of Mount Rushmore, immortalized next to Mr. Lincoln, with all the gum and Lego pieces of my youth.

As the good doctor burrowed deeper through the ascending and descending colon, I began traveling back in time. After the first several feet of colon was revisited like a rerun of *Star Trek*, I began to experience life in my thirties. Oh yes, who could forget the Gallagher's July Fourth barbecue in the mid-1990s? What large intestine could ever pass from memory the agony of all those pork ribs, bucket of coleslaw, topped off by eight Guinness? Onward we traveled. Past my wedding day and drug conviction with their repetitious cavity searches of my mid-twenties. Soon it was the burning returning of my tequila twenty-first birthday. Was it the tacos or the tequila? What a night we all had at the taqueria! Best left unsolved, really. Eventually, we regressed far enough to relive my turbulent toilet training at two and the passing of my meconium stool. Oh, the cramping.

After reliving my passage through the birth canal, I was given the all clear. No polyps, presidents, or parasites. On the way out the good doctor felt obligated to show me close-ups of my internal hemorrhoids. The expression on his face registered both a question and concern. I had dealt with this kind of thing before but couldn't decide whether he was wanting an explanation or a confession. So I gave him both and asked if he found my car keys. After removing the scope, he felt the need to examine my prostate. He gave me a thumbs-up.

Having DJ'd and participated in over five hundred weddings, I've learned two things. The first is that most couples are never really ready to be married. The second is that people preparing for a lifetime of marriage are highly delusional. Most couples getting married are nothing more than glassy-eyed psychotics with a lover's flush. They kiss when one of them leaves. They kiss when one of them returns. They kiss after getting a speeding ticket. They kiss during colonoscopies. The men even talk about their feelings before, during, and after their colonoscopies, then kiss. It all makes me nauseous. Perhaps Oscar Wilde said it best, "Marriage is the triumph of imagination over intelligence." My colonoscopy sure was.

One day your significant other farts in bed, and you finally smell it. It's a little like the tree-falling-in-the-forest analogy. Does it make a noise if no one's there to smell it? Some do. The tapeworm shrugs. Your lover has probably been passing gas in bed for months with you smelling only roses.

But it's an ill wind that blows no good. For gas continues to pass until one is forced to acknowledge not only your partner's bowel afflictions, probably due to tapeworms, but also the crooked teeth, love handles, flabby ass, and tendency to spend too much money. Maybe your wife is a beer drinker and tends to get a little handsy with your friends at wedding receptions after a few cold ones? Maybe you believed your future spouse to be a Los Angeles "ten" a year ago? Only now, you acknowledge that you've been boning nothing more than a "six." So, happy freakin' Valentine's Day.

Whenever I think about being delusional, I think about Willy Wonka. As a boy of six I loved the movie *Willy Wonka & the Chocolate Factory* starring Gene Wilder. I made the mistake of watching Mr. Willy as a really stoned sixteen-year-old. Wow. Yes, through hemp-colored glasses, reefer smoke, and a large pepperoni pizza with mushrooms, the plot thickened.

The real story is that Mr. Wonka is a drug czar. He first goes abroad to "save" the Oompa Loompas from genocide. After winning their confidence, he smuggles the soon-to-be-illegal workers across the border offering freedom, only to make them live and work in his sweatshop he calls a "factory." No one goes in or out, according to Grandpa Joe. Sounds like slave labor to me. From his factory, Mr. Wonka makes and distributes the world's most desirable candy. People can't get enough. Sounds a bit like the crack-cocaine craze of the '90s or the opioid crisis today.

Mr. Wonka hatches a twofold master plan involving the distribution of golden tickets. His randomized ticket offering increases consumption on a global scale, with Mr. Wonka selling more candy than ever. His market share of addiction increases tenfold. But Mr. Wonka's also looking for a prodigy to eventually take over and run his empire. The tickets allow five potential wunderkinds to access his gangster's paradise. Sort of like *The Apprentice*, his gang initiation results in the wannabes getting bumped off one by one due to their own shortcomings in character.

Augustus Gloop is the first to go, doomed by a compulsive eating disorder and mommy issues. Violet Beauregarde suffers from OCD and logorrhea. She overdoses on edibles and is rolled to the emergency room to have her stomach pumped. Bitchy Veruca succumbs to her affluenza and Kardashian-lifestyle obsession, obviously the victim of entitlement. Mike TV suffers from screen addiction and undiagnosed ADHD.

Charlie, the poor but street-smart urchin, passes the final test by returning the designer-drug formula. Like Jesse on *Breaking Bad*, he pledges his misplaced loyalty to Mr. Wonka. Charlie and his family live the rest of their lives in luxury exploiting both the Oompa Loompas and a drug-hungry world. My innocence was lost forever after revisiting that childhood favorite. I didn't need a red pill, like in the *Matrix*, to see reality. All I needed was some Mexican Red Hair Sativa grown in the backyard.

There's nothing wrong with being delusional. God

knows it got me where I am today. The problem is staying there. If only we could.

In order to fulfill my humanities credit for my graduate degree, I took a class titled Marriage and Courtship. After studying this entirely Western notion of romance in depth, or at least enough to get a B minus, I now had scientific data to corroborate my hypothesis. The more memorable research went something like this: generate a whole bunch of videos of a whole bunch of married people and have a whole lot of other married people rate each individual's physical attractiveness and personality. Nobody sees anyone else's ratings. That's called a "blind."

The gist is that married partners rate their own spouses' attractiveness and personality an average of two points higher. There are other factors, such as really knowing someone firsthand and being in love. But just think about it. You think your husband is an "eight," and all the other subjects, both male and female, rate him an average of "six." I'm not talking about a Los Angeles "six" either. I'm talking a Middle America "six," which would be a "four" in most major cities.

Not surprisingly, the longer you're married the more delusional you become. Those together over twenty years are freaking loony toons. Their ratings increased to a three-point difference. Once you get past thirty years of courtship the data becomes difficult to interpret, as older married people start to look and dress alike. Also, divorce, death, and dementia tend to confound the data.

In 1990, when I started my DJ business, the average cost of a hundred-guest wedding on the West Coast was $15,000. In 2019, I DJ'd one of my last weddings, and the average cost that year was $36,000. Now, no one expects to pay the same prices in 2019 as they did in 1990. That would be delusional. But the actual cost in 2019 for the same wedding in 1990, adjusted for inflation, same events, cake, invitations, rings, dresses, etc., comes in at only $22,000. That's right. The rate of inflation says you should be paying $22,000. But you're paying $36,000. $14,000 bought a lot of delusion in 2019.

Truism. Men are the more romantic sex. It's also true that men are generally clueless whether they're getting married or not. They're different sides of the same coin.

I remember a friend from college who could have run the boards on *Jeopardy!*. This guy had an unparalleled memory for factual knowledge. He could recite the entire Constitution and the starting lineups for the New York Yankees and New York Giants from 1901 to the present day. And that's just for starters. He could have made Alex Trebek swoon.

Despite all that brain power, he couldn't put it together that his new wife was fooling around on him. It had started with bizarre dreams about eating giant marsh-mallows. He'd often wake up suffocating, only to find his new wife standing over him holding a large, white pillow.

Soon after the dreams began, his wife's very muscular but previously unbeknownst third cousin, twice removed, bearing no familial resemblance, came to live with them. This family reunion occurred through sheer happenstance. Two distant cousins using the same dating app? What are the chances?

While suffering exhaustion from what he believed was sleep apnea, his wife became eager to reacquaint herself with her distant relation. Soon the two were going out more and more and staying out later and later. Apparently, her distant cousin and now new best friend, really enjoyed the nightlife. Him being new in town and all, what was a cousin to do?

Even after coming home early from work and catching his wife and her third cousin, twice removed, in the shower together, he remained clueless. He believed her story about all those crazy family traditions from Wisconsin. Her husband wasn't dumb, just delusionally in love and wanted to stay there.

His wife eventually divorced him and shacked up with her now nonrelation. My friend was still in love with his ex-wife per our last phone call. He was wanting my advice on another matter altogether, though. A Nigerian prince had emailed him requesting financial assistance in order to get his kingdom back.

Conversely, in the same way that men are clueless about most things, women are predictably clueless when it comes to just one thing—men. Women love a project, which is why I think most of them get married in the first place. What better long-term project for a bride than her groom?

The bride believes that with just the right amount of unsolicited advice, she'll be able to improve her groom and turn him into a misrepresentation of her "dream man." But she forgets that men are clueless to begin with. And that the second flaw of the male species is that they're also very predictable. This leads to a first-order fallacy of the third principle of logic.

A woman will try to use a man's predictability to set him on the road to unsolicited change and self-improvement. However, a man is clueless before he's predictable, so her interventions lead only to predictable cluelessness.

Also, the fact that men are resistant to change in the third place is what makes them so clueless and predictable in the first place. And that's all the answer you'll get from me.

Having at least thought about her wedding day prior to setting the date, a bride will often have very specific ideas and notions. Some have even written scripts and need only insert the name of the groom. Every bride wants her own, share-our-special-day, one-of-a-kind wedding experience. I get that. But thanks to Hollywood and the Bridal Industrial Complex, she becomes progressively more delusional and drifts into predictable cluelessness. Once there, she'll begin creating her own one-of-a-kind dream wedding based on her three favorite wedding movies. Art doesn't imitate life, it romanticizes it.

One bride, after seeing *The Wedding Singer*, *My Best Friend's Wedding*, and *Mamma Mia* added her own predictable spin that produced one flashy, flaring, flamboyant event. It was easy enough to find a crooner to sing out of tune ala Adam Sandler. The problem that she experienced was finding the Rupert Everett character, the gay, oh-so-very-empathetic best friend she never had in college to complete the screenplay.

Her vision was not a unique one. I have no doubt that any male actor willing to play the part of Rupert during the 1990s and early 2000s could have cleaned up. He'd shamelessly set up at the bridal show sandwiched between the Have Your Cake and Eat It Too bakery and the Lovey Dovey Lingerie Emporium. "Available for hire, gay best friend of the bride, no relationship history necessary, $200 an hour."

The bride, in this case, was forced to accept one of

her maid of honors' very muscular but previously unbeknownst third cousin, twice removed, bearing no familial resemblance. With *Mamma Mia* finishing the list of the three, the bride had to settle for Greek fries, not Greek guys, while dancing to ABBA's "Dancing Queen."

I'll toss the brides a bouquet here. At age seventeen, I affectatiously believed that Molly Ringwald was my forever true love. After watching the *Breakfast Club* for the hundredth time, I knew she was meant for me. As the outro movie theme by Simple Minds began to play, I was the one kissing Molly, not Judd Nelson. I was hopelessly, delusionally in love. In reality, while I was watching the closing credits at the local cineplex, Molly was looking pretty in pink for Andrew McCarthy.

The kicker in all this is that after the delusion wears off, the movie credits roll, the spin of Hollywood winds down, married or not, couples still decide to stay together. You may wake up one day to a farting, tapeworm-infected partner and decide you still love them. The internal parasite, not so much. Even after the facade of romantic love tumbles like the walls of Jericho, brought down by the roar of your partner's incessant snoring, you stay. You stay!

Years from now, I'll probably be married to the same wonderful person. She will always be an LA "nine" in my eyes, regardless of future data indicating she's a Middle America "six."

Before long, I'll be back on the colonoscopy table for another exposé of my large colon. However vain I may still be, I hope to relive again the wonderful past my partner and I have shared together. Only this time more slowly and hopefully less painfully. Once again, I'll choose to remain conscious.

From the moment the good doctor passes the point of no return and instructs his assistant to push the scope over my right hepatic flexures, I hope to know. Or, maybe it will be the near puncturing of my right lung that will bring everything into crystalline focus. Why, am I still in love?

WHAT THE
BRIDESMAID SAW

S HE WAS LATE. No call, no text, no email. I gave her a ring at fifteen after. Nothing, voicemail full. The headache of being stood up I didn't need. What I wanted was some peace and quiet. I'd planned to spend the afternoon with a couple friends. The first I kept in a CD case, name was Miles. My other friend I kept in a bottle, pinot noir. The dame needed to meet with me today, the urgency in her voice obvious. I was here. But where was she? All the necessary paperwork was ready to go on the table in front of me. I was a wedding DJ, it said so on my business cards.

The facts were few. Through her scattered stream of consciousness and broken cell phone reception, I worked it out that she was in deep trouble. She needed a wedding DJ fast. What I wanted were more facts. But what I needed was a drink.

She came into the coffee shop like a windmill caught in a tornado, dragging some goon behind her. So, the bride with the baby blues was bringing a little muscle to help work the deal, eh? A second look turned over all the cards. The lost expression on the young man's mug could only mean one thing—he was the groom. I'd seen this utterly clueless look too many times not to miss it. I decided to play it cool.

When working a case it was sometimes best to see the couple in their natural environment. They stepped to the counter. She ordered a quadruple, 110-degree, double mocha, hold the whipped cream. I didn't hear what the groom ordered but watched the barista pull three espresso shots and poor them into a shorty. They shared a look meant only for lovers. Yep, they were in love, all right. I rolled those dice a few times myself. Shot a lot of craps before finally rolling a seven. Although they both looked harried, they had the glow of having had satisfying morning coitus. After receiving her drink, the bride drank half of it down in a single swig. This seemed to take some of the wind out of her sails. But when I see a woman drink like that I know she's near the breaking point. The groom appeared less clueless and more reflective sipping his three-shot ristretto. I took a sip of black coffee. Maybe I could work with these two.

Blowing my cover, I raised my hand, followed by a bus-driver nod, finishing with a toothy grin. They must not have seen me because they turned and went the other direction. They first visited the booth closest to the door, approaching a serious-looking man sitting alone sipping a vanilla latte. He appeared slighted and alarmed by the idea of being mistaken for a wedding DJ. He shook his head, a definite no. At a glance I knew the man's business. He was a stationer. Eventually they'd find their way to my table. They always did. I decided to sit this one out and let the client do some detective work for a change.

After checking every booth in the place they made their way to me. The bride approached. "DJ Chris?" Her inflection indicated both a question and concern. I'd dealt with this kind of thing before. I'd been using sunscreen over the last several years, per my dermatologist's request. My snow-white tan combined with my gray hair and natural good looks was sometimes just too much for the ladies. I nodded and showed them the other side of the booth.

I asked the couple how I could help. Before Miss Baby Blues could open her mouth the waterworks started. Through the tsunami of tears I made the story front page. Her situation was dire. The catering company, the photographer, and her grandmother from Poughkeepsie were all showing up for a wedding reception. The catch? No DJ. The bum she'd hired and paid in full a year ago wrote her a Dear Joan letter that arrived two days ago. The DJ returned the fee in cash and a letter saying he couldn't play the wedding—get this—due to family matters. Nothing else. She tried to call him, but the louse had changed his number. The letter was short and to the point, like the knife that had been pushed into her heart. The bastard. Letters like that come first class, just like the jerks who send them.

Then she dropped her own punchline. The wedding was set for... today! Ceremony at five, reception to follow. She was due for makeup and hair in forty-five minutes. Pictures were set for an hour after that. The groom still had to pick up his tux and family from the airport in the limousine. The DJ they'd hired had agreed to play the reception but at half my going fee. They had a maestro playing classical guitar for the ceremony at the church. I caught a break there. A mere $300 was all they had. Across the table I saw the waterworks beginning again. She had me. I agreed to do it, but we had to do it my way, or no way at all.

No time for an agenda now. I needed to load the equipment, change, and get to the venue to set up. I told the couple we'd discuss their canary songs later. What we needed now was action. Driving home, I ripped all the pages out of my rule book and left them on the pavement behind me. Was I crazy or just getting soft? Maybe some crazy is what was needed to pull this thing off. Turning into my driveway it hit me that maybe I wasn't doing the gig for just the couple and three hundred clams?

The wife met me at the door. She had the face of an angel contemplating my sin. Before going to meet with the couple, the two of us had planned on spending the evening together, with both us of wanting to roll lucky sevens in the romance department. This postman always rings twice, but the new lines on my face told her all she didn't want to know. Our "tango in Paris" would have to wait. I was going to work, and she knew I meant business. She knew better than to complain, and I knew it was best to keep my mouth shut and get on with the job.

After I finished loading my rig, she gave me a kiss and a sandwich. I handed her the pile of cash. She stuffed the Jacksons inside her bra. She'd hold them next to her heart until I got back. I considered it an investment. When I got home, we might still hit it big and both payoff in silver dollars. I'd realized long ago that some us just weren't meant for gold. My friends Miles and pinot would have to wait.

After driving thirty minutes to the hotel, I joined the circus. Today, everyone was selling tickets. The hotel hosted *six* banquet rooms. I'd played them all at least a dozen times. Six weddings tonight, filling all the rooms and all the parking. The load/unload zone was lined up till next Tuesday, with all the other hacks with their thumbs in the matrimonial pie. Unloading now were the caterers for room four. These circus clowns would take at least an hour to unload the "big top" they brought along. Two other vendors were waiting in line behind them. To pull this wedding off, I'd need a little luck and a favor.

Parking in the space marked "Security Only" I made my way to the door. I smiled at the camera focusing on the entrance. Phil was working. I could tell by the paranoid way the camera zoomed in and out of focus. Holding up one of the twenties I'd lifted from my wife's bra during our last embrace, I palmed it to the camera, showing Jackson's best side. Nothing. The bill found my pocket. I pulled out one of the only two photographs in my wallet. I palmed the senior picture of my younger sister into the camera's view. The autofocus zoomed in, detailing the photograph. Yeah, that Phil was a nervous bastard, all right. The security door buzzed; I was in.

Meeting Phil for the first time was a lot like visiting Australia. Great country, nice folks, but the wildlife should have disappeared a million years ago. Instead of giving up their space for evolution and higher life forms, they just got busy getting a little more inbred. Phil looked a bit like the platypus. A combination of a lot of things that evolutionarily should have died long ago. At his best he looked like a jigsaw puzzle with a couple pieces missing.

He greeted me at the top of the stairs outside the security monitoring room. I gave him my hand. He shook it the way someone makes popcorn using a flamethrower. I asked him how it was going, but now it was my turn to sweat. He'd fancied my sister since the second grade and had fallen for her the way a pebble does in the Grand Canyon—long and hard. I knew my angle and my play, but anybody could tell this *Beauty and the Beast* fairytale would end just like it had for Fae Rae and King Kong. Phil didn't see it, though. To him, a date with my sister was a chance for something better. Maybe something better was what we all wanted.

I told him about why I was there. I needed the security-only parking space for the evening in order to pull off the caper. He nodded the way someone does when they understand what you're saying but don't necessarily agree. He asked if my youngest sister happened to be single. I replied in the affirmative, that she currently was, and left it at that. I needed the spot fast, so I gave the bee a little more honey. Nancy was on the rebound, I told him. What followed was a half-true story about her getting dumped by Nick the garbage man. The true story was that Nancy had dumped him for two-timing her with a third-class waitress at a second-hand diner down on First Street. I assured him I'd call her tomorrow and put in a good word about how good Phil was looking and then maybe, *maybe,* she'd go out with him. He said he needed her number up front to make the deal work. I was desperate to secure the parking spot, so I gave him her new number.

He'd call her three days later, after thinking long and hard about all he wanted to say. He always did. My sister would call me immediately after she screened his call to tear me a new one. Like the fleabag I was, I'd take it lying down while sipping some pinot.

The hotel was busier than a busty beaver breakdancing in a beehive. My negotiation with Phil ate more time off the clock than I anticipated, and I was no way near ready to launch. I ran in my three CD cases and put them on the skirted DJ table. Back out again. Throwing the two mains on top of the sub with wheels, I pushed it up the ramp. Left it next to the DJ table and went back for the rest: speaker stands, cords, CD changer, laptop. Slowing it down this time to catch my breath, I had a chance to peek into a few of the other rooms on the way down the hall. It was a goddamned DJ gala, starring all the usual players.

Pretty Boy Byron Jones in ballroom one. Soul Train D'Wayne in two. Three and four were split by the Hansen brothers. They were twins, so alike that even their own mother couldn't tell them apart. But when it comes to playing music, no two DJs spin the same. The older twin was more old school. He favored the 1970s and '80s classics, maybe a little too much. His younger brother just loved to bang the gong around and played louder and heavier than anyone I knew. With four subwoofers, who wouldn't? To my right, room five was still being prepped. I was in ballroom six; it said so above the door.

I had less than thirty minutes to create a little wedding magic. How many times had I set it all up, five hundred? Seven hundred? A thousand? A green-eyed cutie of a bridesmaid dressed in pink ran in to tell me the guests were arriving. I hit the play button on the CD changer and started the show off with a playlist of my own. The CD featured various artists, a little something for everybody.

The pretty dame was right. Guests trickled in with the couple supposedly mere minutes behind. We had nothing on paper, and they still didn't have a first dance or the inkling of what they wanted as far as reception events. It was going to be a long night.

Before I could collect my thoughts, Ms. Pretty in Pink was back bending my ear.

She gave me the dope, straight, no chaser. Sitting outside in the limo, the newly married couple was close to melting down. I told her to keep them on ice while I came up with a plan to avoid Chernobyl. To the guests, I made a short announcement that the bar was opening early. All the tap beer and wine you could drink was on the house. This should keep the natives from getting restless and buy a little more time.

The limo was easy to spot. It was the one that looked like a crime scene. The bridal party and both sets of parents were standing around giving bad advice. My experience? Your father may be giving you away at the wedding, and maybe he taught you how to catch a trout or ride your first two-wheeler, but fathers of the bride should save the advice for after the wedding when the couple is considering financial planning or buying that first home. But nobody was asking me.

Mothers are more sympathetic the day of the wedding. Most get trapped, though, in their own nostalgic past, vicariously trying to relive the memories from their wedding day. Even with the best of intentions, most matriarchs flounce around causing confusion, like the female protagonist in a Jane Austen novel. The couple wasn't reading any self-help books, that was for sure. I didn't see a single copy of *How to Get Your Shit Together and Get Your Ass Out of the Limo*. So, like usual, I stuck my mug in where it didn't belong. Inside the limo, the waterworks were flowing again, and even the groom wiped a wet one from the corner of his eye. They were going to pieces, big time. I needed to quiet all the noise. I'd seen the photographer enter the hall after I made the announcement for free hooch. I told the family that the photographer needed them all inside for a picture, everybody except the couple. They beat it. I finally had the couple alone.

Both of them started down the list of what was going wrong. Like the crack of a .38, I cut them short with a loud *Hey!* It resonated with a finality that made all three of us blush. They looked up, indignant by my blunt retort, but it put a kibosh on the crying game. It was the slap across the face they both needed, and it gave me an opening.

First thing I said, "We need to get you in the hall so we can get the show going." I asked if they liked the musical group Journey, and they both mumbled yes. I turned to the groom. "Your last name Johnson?" A quick nod. All right, then. I had a song, and they were the Johnsons. Pretty in Pink was coming back to check on the couple. I told them we were doing the announcement of the couple and told the bridesmaid to hang close as I needed her for my cue outside the ballroom.

Back to the DJ station to start them on their reception "journey." Dumping the volume to about a third, I got the guests involved quickly by putting their hands together for the couple's entrance. With a few nudges they reached the volume of applause I wanted. The lubrication from the open bar was already greasing the wheels. I gave the nod for Pretty in Pink to bring in the couple. She stopped outside the door, and the crowd welcomed Mr. and Mrs. Johnson into their reception. The crowd started singing as "Don't Stop Believin'" hit its first chorus. Hugs and kisses all around. No time to lose. I pulled aside the best man and had him poor half a draft each, no more, for the bride and groom. They were looking better but still needed to loosen up. We had a lot of work to do, and I needed them to stay frosty.

After sipping their beers, I made my way over to the couple. They seemed more relaxed but still anxious. In a nicer tone I told them we'd open the buffet in twenty minutes having already checked with the caterers. As a DJ, you never ask, you tell. So I told, nicely. No protesting this time, just a nod. I knew we could work together.

We opened the buffet, wedding couple first. I gave the Johnsons another half drink each, on top of some alfredo and Caesar salad. Then we'd plan the toasts and cake cutting. They were doing fine, but I didn't want to push too hard, too fast. Sometimes you have to walk before you can run. During the downtime I was able to put together a playlist as well as a few discs for the dancing. Later, I got the crowd to applaud the couple a second time just for being so damn cute. We'd be excusing by table in minutes.

While writing down notes for the bouquet toss and garter toss, Pretty in Pink touched my shoulder. I turned, expecting a question, but received only an answer. She'd brought me a glass of vino, wanting to thank me for all the help in getting the Johnsons out of the double-parked limo and into the reception. I cut a half smile, as if to say "All part of the job, toots." Her eyes were green. Lips the color of the wine in my glass. As she walked back to the head table I noticed she carved a nice figure. She knew who and what she was. I took a sip. It was pinot.

After dinner we had the toasts. I reviewed proper mic

technique with the maid of honor and best man and got the low down on who was speaking and who wasn't. The champagne, per my cue, was already being passed around. We were set to go. I had the couple stand next to their head table. No reason to move newlyweds unless we had to. After quieting the crowd, I got the best man into position.

Most people freak when they first hear their voice over a PA, and this best man was no exception. He lowered the mic immediately after starting his speech. Like lightning, I was on it and quickly caught his arm, raising the mic back up to his mouth. He started in again with his speech, lowering the mic a second time. I made an exaggerated grab toward the microphone, with him snatching it up on his own. We both laughed, along with the room. It came off like a rehearsed comedy bit, with me playing the clown. Nice. He kept the speech short and sweet. Glasses up, and we toasted.

The maid of honor was next. She had a nice voice and knew her way around a microphone. She'd known the bride since first grade. She went on about the ancient history for what seemed like a century. When she got to the college years, she started flowing like Niagara Falls. I'd seen ladies in waiting lose it before, but this flood was on par with Noah's. Eventually, she brought it back. They always do. She dried her eyes and raised her glass and toasted the couple.

We'd made it over the halfway mark. All we had left was the first dance and a few other niceties. I'd run the show after that until we sent the couple home at midnight. Piece of wedding cake. I felt a now familiar touch on my shoulder. It was Pretty in Pink. She wasn't bringing me any pinot this time. What she brought was the final piece in this puzzle. She bent my ear that the DJ setting up across the hall had been the one who'd pulled out last minute on her sister. Pretty had been there at the bridal show when her sister had paid in full. Peeking into room five, I knew that Liberace smile instantly—it was the King.

The King and I had a history. We went way back and had our moments with, and at, each other. Just like the Cold War, bringing out our big guns meant mutually assured destruction for everybody. Nobody would win or get a tip at the end of the night. We'd backed off the escalation a few years prior. I'd make nice for now.

What was his mug doing here anyway? And setting up so late on a Saturday? The alarm went off in my head like a 1960s duck-and-cover drill. It was July, the seventh month, the seventh day of the month, and in the year 2007. Ceremony start time for the King's wedding was seven.

The King had booked the Johnson wedding over a year ago because they were paying in full, and he needed cash. Only later did he put it together that the date 07/07/07 was worth a lot more than three hundred clams. He canceled last minute due to a shortage of DJs for the most requested date in a millennium. He'd played them all as chumps and strong-armed the couple with the most dough. All along, the future Johnsons were set to play the patsy. He probably rolled the desperate couple in his room for at least two grand.

Now I knew why this wedding was about more than the bride with the baby-blue eyes and the three hundred clams. It was about me and the King squaring off for the last time. He'd broken the one code of being a wedding DJ that I'd never cross—he sold out a couple after being paid in full in order to take another gig for more money. Bastard. Family matters, eh? The King seemed to be handling the death of his late mother just fine. He was now dead in my eyes and would be finished when the word got out, which I'd make sure it would. No wedding planner, caterer, photographer, bartender, couple, or fellow DJ would recommend him ever again after they found out what he'd done.

Those working within the Bridal Industrial Complex have a code. We would sell each other out at the drop of a hat to get a gig, but you never went back on a wedding deal after you took the money, no matter how sweet the coin was for the next offer.

A lesson taught needed to be a lesson learned. I thought about Mrs. Baby Blues (now married) crying in the rain at the coffee shop. Now, we were getting ready to cut the cake. If what I had in mind panned out, the King would be eating humble pie for years to come.

After the cake cutting, I powwowed with the couple to choose the first dance. I had the selection they had been thinking about. The Johnson's were a long way from Fred Astaire and Ginger Rogers, so I'd invite all the guests out to join them after the first chorus. To ease the anxiety, I recommended that the couple combine the father-daughter and mother-son dances. Relief all the way around. The groom gave me a side hug, Mrs. Baby Blues kissed me on the cheek. Pretty in Pink was behind them smiling wider than the Jordan River. Christ, she had nice gams. Later, she brought me over a second glass of pinot.

Placing my hand on top of hers, I told her no. We'd drink the pinot together when it was all over.

Between spinning discs at my own event, I was working Phil hard. I told him the whole convoluted story about the King and the now newly married Mrs. Baby Blues. Phil was a softy at heart despite looking like a platypus. After wiping away a few tears, he was onboard.

I called in a few favors and promised a free Christmas party to one particular professional I knew outside the bridal business. The head maître d' working at the hotel was sympathetic to my cause and found me an extra jacket. His run-ins with the King had been similar to mine.

Everything was in place by the time we got to the open dancing in my ballroom. My couple was doing great. Mrs. Baby Blues was smiling ear to ear while dancing with her loving husband. We could dethrone the King, but I'd need a little help from Pretty in Pink.

She was a quick learner and knew her part well. I needed her to keep the King distracted while I borrowed his car keys. One minute was all I needed to pull this off. If the King had a chink in his coiffed, manicured armor, it was his vanity. Like most DJs, he also had a soft spot for the ladies.

Before she went in to see the King, I watched her loosen the halter straps on her bridesmaid dress and peel off her pumps. She began twirling her shoes like they were fur dice hanging over the dash of a 1965 Mustang GT on a bumpy road. She walked toward the King, feigning the slightest tipsy stagger, which added to the bounce in her bosom. She was also carrying a glass of pinot. Pretty approached the King by his blind side, leaving his back to me so I could enter unnoticed. She cooed to the King that she needed someone to stir her drink. Without asking, she placed the King's finger in her glass, giving it a swirl, before placing the wine-soaked finger in her mouth. She had his attention and my admiration.

DJs are superstitious bastards. They set up their table exactly the same each time. The CD changer to the left, playlist to the right, microphone just so—you know the story. Per my previous encounters with the King, I knew he kept his car keys in the left pocket of his suit jacket. He was in the habit of jingling them when he was feeling cocky, which was always. While she was getting him hot, I noticed the jacket on the back of the chair closest to me. Feigning a busboy bow to pick up an imaginary napkin, I lifted the keys and raced down the hall to the parking lot to find the King's car. I had a gift for him.

A quick look around the parking lot told me things were falling in line. My part would make this personal and put the final decoration on the King's bon voyage party. I locked his car and ran back to the ballroom. The electric slide was finishing up in my room, and time was winding down fast. I needed to drop the monkey suit and get back to being DJ Chris so I could keep my alibi. I looked in on the King to make the switch and got blind-sided. The King was wearing his jacket.

Even the King could make my mug close range through this thin disguise. I made a desperate attempt to get directly behind him, bowing once again for imaginary napkins. I'd bump him and put the keys in his pocket. Pretty in Pink had been reading my mind and pretended to fall all over the King, flashing more than her green eyes. He reached out to catch her; they always did. Pretty was laying it on thick, her cleavage now supplying the full-court press I needed to get the King to drop the zone coverage and go man-to-man. The keys were now back in the left pocket with the King none the wiser. Running into room six, I lost the hotel jacket and became DJ Chris again.

It was the witching hour. July 7 was now July 8. All the necessary players were assembled in the viewing room, courtesy of Phil. He'd broken all the rules letting outsiders into the hotel's security operations, the secret inner sanctum. Here the hotel kept the dirty secrets on guests and staff alike. Phil was the one handling the home movies and proud of the live event he was about to preview for us. We had all taken chances and done our part to frame the King. Pretty in Pink was standing next to me, smiling proudly. She was good, real good. We watched it go down on the video screens courtesy of Phil and cameras one, two, and three.

The King was getting ready to load out. He hadn't been to his car since his reception had started. Now it was time for a little payback. The King walked out to his car only to see a ticket pinned to the windshield. It was for parking in a handicapped spot. Three hundred fifty clams payable to the good people of the County. The policeman was still there sniffing around the car, paying particular attention to the rear license plate. Tabs were a year out of date. Four hundred fifty clams. The King began yacking. We could see his lips flapping, all right. He was trying to play dumb to the whole thing, but the cop wasn't buying it.

Then the flatfoot saw something he didn't like in the back seat. It was a half bottle of hooch. In the eyes of the officer, this man was preparing to drive his car with an open bottle of wine in reach of the driver. Three hundred clams. The officer got closer to the King and said he smelled a whole lot of juniper berries. He asked the King if he'd been drinking gin. Does a Bigfoot crap in the woods? I knew exactly what the cop was saying, because I was the one who'd written it.

I watched the show up until the cavity search. The evening would eventually cost the King over three thousand bucks and ruin his reputation all over town. While turning to go, I was pulled into the dark office behind me. Before I could swear, Pretty in Pink was all over me, like a windmill in a tornado. I responded to her like a man, being a man, being a man with a woman. Oh man! I knew it was wrong, but her mouth was hungry and passionate with fresh-fruit notes and scents of raspberry, blackberry, and cherry. Coming up to breathe, I caught floral notes of rose, peony, and violet. Her bosom was glowing like the metal on the edge of a knife. My own private Idaho, with twin moons rising over a new hope.

You can talk about forbidden fruit and Adam and Eve all you want. She was half my age. My god, how the heavens played with the hearts of mortals. But she was meant for more than a midnight tryst of redemption at the lips of an aging wedding DJ. I knew after kissing her that she was pure gold. I broke the kiss and pulled my hands from her bosom... eventually. I told her that the two of us didn't amount to a hill of beans in this world and that she was meant for a far, far better life than I could give her. So, I had to let her go. She said okay and walked over to put a lip-lock on Phil.

Driving home, I played the night over in my mind.

The Johnsons had pulled it together and the reception was a success. The plot to dethrone the King was simple. Phil had changed the sign in front of the King's parking spot from "Wedding Vendor" to a handicapped parking sign. On his smoke break, the maître d' had peeled off the current year sticker on the King's license plate with his stiletto. I placed the half bottle of pinot in his backseat to add a personal touch. As for the cop being in the right place at the right time? Let's just say the big brother of another little sister screwed over by the King just happened to be patrolling the area. The kissy-kissy-lover-boy ending with Pretty in Pink went round and round in my head.

The wife met me at the door. Her face was that of an angel contemplating my sin. My mug told her what she already knew and maybe what she didn't want to know. So, what about our tango in Paris? She slowly unbuttoned her sequined blouse to the navel before letting it drop. As her lace bra hit the floor, the twenties tumbled down like dice thrown at a craps game. Yeah, we knew each other the way a silver dollar knows a pocket. Loose change was the way we always played it. Long ago, we both realized that some of us weren't meant for gold. My friends Miles and pinot would have to wait a little longer.

THE AUTHOR

T*HE WEDDING DJ's Diary* is Christopher's first literary venture! He's hoping to sell lots of books so he can afford to update the above picture. In the photograph, Christopher is looking offstage to see his muse, which only appeared on school-picture day, much to the exasperation of his mother. Future works in progress include the novella *Polar Bears, Suicide, and Hot Yoga.* The story is a classic tragedy or comedy, depending on whether the author adds punchlines, in which boy meets polar bear, boy loses polar bear, boy meets girl, love story? He's also working diligently on his next series of essays, which provide a distraught, dysfunctional digression into his childhood, titled *The Woodland Avenue Confidential.* Anyone wanting to adapt his work to a Netflix Original series, feel free to call.

"I like that DJ Chris guy. He has a detached view of the world. Kind of like everything is just a big joke."

—ED BERGER, ANONYMOUS NEIGHBOR, WOODLAND AVENUE

"Those experiencing childhood trauma will often trivialize the horror. I hope the author can begin picking away at the scabs of his emotional wounds and shed his persona of indifference and false bravado elucidated in his writing and finally get honest with himself."

—DR. DAVID FRIEND, CHILD PSYCHIATRIST

"When I read the essay, 'The Chicken Bone,' it was like I was there choking on the post-wedding buffet. You might think there's nothing funny about someone choking, but just wait until you read this book. And I'm sure just about everyone can relate to the selection 'On the Third Day, He Rested,' but most of us don't look at it quite the way the author does. I enjoyed this book from start to finish, and you will too."

—DR. TODD, EDUCATIONAL CONSULTANT

"Loved the book. I'm intrigued by the author's refined belief in the existence of 'Nessy,' otherwise known as the Loch Ness Monster. As the human spokesman for Nessy and all creatures residing within the loch, I extend a hardy salutation. Now, let's talk about sewage. If I've told the travel industry once, I've told them a thousand times not to encourage the tourists to pee in the lake. The concentration of human urine in the loch during the summer months can reach intoxicating levels for both Nessy and the local fish stocks. Also, a horrible stench wafts up from the public beaches in mid-August. Pee-yew. Something must be done, and adult diapers should never enter the picture. Save us from ourselves. Oh, Nessy..."

—WIZARD NARCAN ROSEWOOD, THE NESSY PRESERVATION PROJECT, SCOTLAND

"Chris was always a great friend growing up. Cool guy, nice tush. I think he danced or something. Haven't seen him since the 1990s. My art loft just isn't the same without his good-looking legs around. I told him print was dead... butt... ass..."

—BYRON JONES, ARTIST AND LOFT OWNER

"Does this guy have a real job? Maybe someone at a public school will give him a job in the lunchroom?"

—MATT HELM, JANITOR, WOODLAND
AVENUE ELEMENTARY

"As a former stationer, I take exception to Mr. Bartness's stereotyped portrayal of my profession. Yes, we're all good spellers, unlike the author. Apparently, Mr. Bartness never uses vocabulary that would require one to open a dictionary. Stationers are not serious all the time. We have parties and occasionally cut loose."

—RICHARD KNOBB, LAW PARTNER

"Mr. Bartness's writing is the literary equivalent of a burger and fries purchased off the dollar menu. A great book for the nonreader."

—AL SMITHY, BOOK REVIEWER

"I know Bigfoot is for real. My fiancé and I were having coitus twenty miles out on Five Mile Road. I happened to look up between changing CDs from AC/DC to Hank Williams Jr. when I saw a herd of Bigfoots coming out of the darkness. Lucky for us we were driving a '65 Mustang GT, not my mom's bogus Malibu. DJ Chris is cool, spun discs at my second wedding."

—PARKER LEE, BIGFOOT ENTHUSIAST,
FORMER BRIDE

"DJ Chris rips the virginal veil right off the Bridal Industrial Complex and exposes the seedy underbelly within."

—J. JILL, BLOGGER AND FORMER SEX THERAPIST

"People suffering from anger issues are just the same as everyone else. Okay, so we get a little hot on occasion and throw small children in the ditch. Well, excuse me! You try growing up on Woodland Avenue and see how you turn out! It's all picnics and parades on the outside, but below the surface you feel like a Bigfoot trapped in a piñata, always hoping that the children never break through to get your candy. Oh my God! I'm so pissed right now!"

—DEAN KEMPER, WOODLAND AVENUE'S FORMER RESIDENT BULLY

"This author is an asshole."

—PETER BURNS, ARBITRARY BOOKS AND PRESIDENT OF TOASTMASTERS

"I remember dancing to the jams of DJ Chris on several occasions. Great DJ. Great look. Kinda had that Johnny Winter vibe going on. It was nice to see a public figure celebrating his albinism, and at his advanced age, too. Heard him play some jazz bass downtown. That cat can swing."

—DAVID SWEET, BASSIST FOR THE NOT SO AVERAGE WHITE BAND

"For F--*-sake, I just hope this isn't a trilogy."*

—OLD LUMBER BOOKS

"They just kept coming at me with those pointy tails. I tried to get away from the marmots or groundhogs or whatever they were. They finally sandwiched me next to the buffet table, poking me at will. I finally gave in. Then the three of us slow danced to 'Muskrat Love.' I bought my first breeding pair of guinea pigs the next day."

—DAREN, *GROUNDHOG DAY* MOVIE ENTHUSIAST AND GUINEA PIG BREEDER

"The growth of this author can only be measured by a Mayan Calendar."

—BIFF "WE DON'T TALK ANYMORE" RICHARDS, BROKEN HEART BOOKS

"DJ Chris is being oh so clever drawing comparison between one's preference in costume play and making inferences regarding one's sexual proclivities. As a licensed sex therapist, I often recommend that couples use costume and fantasy play in order to enhance their sexual experiences and increase intimacy. My current partner and I will often incorporate costumes into our sexual repertoire. I remember one particularly satisfying evening in February 1999 where we both dressed like groundhogs. A good time was had by all."

—ANONYMOUS SEX THERAPIST

"Chris is a really good guy. He tried kissing me once at a junior high dance... like kissing a sea cucumber dipped in molasses. After twenty years of therapy, I can finally eat seafood again. Lousy kisser but a really good guy. He should stick to writing, though. Love you!"

—MONIQUE MARQUE-FABER, FORMER
GIRLFRIEND (FOR THREE DAYS)

"I can't believe the author sold that many books. There's one born every minute. Mr. Bartness must have access to a preschool, exploiting the nonreader."

—BRAD KOBAIN, SECOND-GRADE
TEACHER AND GUITAR PLAYER

"I remember meeting DJ Chris when I was a child. We'd just moved to Washington State from Central America. He was so white my brother and sister thought he was the abominable snowman. In my elementary school we came to know him as 'Muy Blanco.' My parents later explained that anyone that white must have severe anemia. We all ate our liver and onions without question after that. My neighbor called the ambulance twice, hoping to get the author some badly needed healthcare before he collapsed. This is why I ask for your vote. Please support healthcare for all, including the author."

—RICARDO GIUTERZ, STATE LEGISLATURE, DEMOCRAT

"I danced with DJ Chris on numerous occasions. It's really true what they say about how one's style of dancing reflects their actions in the bedroom. Let's just say DJ Chris dances like a washing machine with a broken spin cycle. Miss your dancer's butt. Call me!"

—JULIE MORGAN, CWU ALUM AND FRIEND

"I had more fun reading this book than a bride on her wedding night, at least on my wedding night anyway. Brad had a few too many. I especially liked the essay 'What the Bridesmaid Saw.' His retelling from the bridesmaid's point of view was authentic, raw, and honest!"

—MEGAN SMITH, EDUCATIONAL CONSULTANT, AND SEX THERAPIST

"The essays are refreshingly witty and bring the reader right up to the wedding altar. In a page-turning confidential, Bartness illustrates through hilarious anecdotes the hypocrisy of the Bridal Industrial Complex. You won't regret spending a weekend with a glass of wine and his book of wonderful prose. Just say I do—I did!"

—SARA MARKLE-VINTER, PROFESSIONAL POODLE GROOMER

"The Wedding DJ's Diary provides humor, drama, and tantalizing twists and turns making it the perfect bedside companion. Lucky readers who purchase his book will never again be unprepared for any wedding eventuality."

—MAGARETT MEAD

"His one essay, 'The Bride, the Groom, and the Wardrobe,' reminded me of a story I read as a kid... I just can't place it. Yep, seemed really familiar. It brought me back to my own wedding-day wardrobe malfunction. One of the essays in the middle is kinda confusing, but I really liked Andy Gibb growing up."

—TRACY STARR, *SKAGIT BEACON*

"A better name for this book would be The Wedding DJ's Diarrhea... shit in, shit out. Pathetic prose says it best."

—DR. EUGENE, LITERARY PROFESSOR

"I'm so proud. I remember watching him play with his crayons the first day of kindergarten. He was so fond of coloring. I like that Chris is still working on his writing skills, but some of his writing seems sloppy. I give his first book an A for effort."

—MRS. HARRIS, KINDERGARTEN TEACHER

"Great writing for a bass player, man! Reading his book brought me back to the '80s like a game of Pac-Man. I didn't know he could write. He got most of the story straight when talking about the band."

—ZEKE, DRUMMER AND LIBERTARIAN CANDIDATE

"It's like he just nails the whole wedding thing, you know? It's crazy, but fun, when you don't even know it, right? Those stories could have been about me... I mean, I played Pac-Man..."

—ANONYMOUS BRIDE

"Thinking of the perfect Christmas gift? Look no further. I'm going to buy one for everyone and anyone on my shopping list. Well written. A great read! I love the nostalgic view of the author. A real gem. As a minister, I think I'll give a book to each couple I marry."

—KAREN, MINISTER OF UNIVERSALIST CHURCH

"He was a great wedding DJ for our June Mamma Mia extravaganza. Showed up on time, very professional. He looked old and a little tired, though, maybe anemic? Come to think of it, he was one the whitest people I've ever seen. His essay 'Mommy Dearest' was a great read!"

—FRANK, ANONYMOUS GROOM

"I read the book... like doing a keg stand with light beer."

—BOBBY, GROOMSMAN

"*Great series of essays, loved them all. I would like, however, to talk to Mr. Bartness about an unsolved arson in the mid-1990s at the old metal works downtown. Seems funny to me he'd mention pyromania in one essay and discuss arson in a second, then have the metal works burn down in a third... almost like he was giving himself an alibi.*"

—Detective Smith

"*This writer is deeper than the Mariana Trench. His insight into the folly of the human experience is brilliant. His absence from the literary world thus far has been a loss. Hopefully, 'The Master' Mr. Bartness will keep writing and educating those oblivious to the obvious.*"

—P. T. Barium, Libertarian Candidate

"*When I think about this book, I think about Christmas or the circus. Either way, it's about giving. Anyone who reads this book should buy at least ten or so copies to give to friends and relatives at Christmas or Easter or birthdays or just anytime. I think it's all about value. And let me tell you, this book is the real deal. I love the author's analysis of two of my favorite childhood Disney films. Bartness rocks!*"

—Mary Anne S., Slap Shot Books

"This is a book for the person who's really ready to examine who they are and where they want to go in life."

—B. HASCALL, LIFE COACH

"Finally, a book for the little guy who makes good. Mr. Bartness takes a look at the human condition, then transcends all you've ever known or ever will know to the pure existence in his multiversed essays. A fun read!"

—A. RASCAL, PACKRAT BOOKS

"This is the only book I ever read. I sleep with it each night. Just this morning I woke up with it stuck to my forehead!"

—PATRICIA POST, FORMER GIRLFRIEND, HIGH SCHOOL ALUM, AND COUNTY JUDGE

"References to sexuality in this book are based on worn-out clichés and stereotyping. Mr. Bartness thinks he's being clever in 'Groom Up!' using colors to describe sexual proclivities. I hope the literary community will avoid reading this tripe like the perverted plague it is. To quote the author, 'It all started with the crayons.' After reading this collection, it makes one ponder whether it should have ended there as well."

—SECOND ANONYMOUS SEX THERAPIST

"Haven't seen this much fluff since I last sheared my golden doodle."

—CAMANO SENTINEL

"Laughed, cried, and stopped reading after five pages. I returned the book at half value."

—ANOTHER SATISFIED BIBLIOPHILE

"You'll be using a pen name, right?"

—THE WIFE

"For his essay 'Groom Up!' just a two-word review: 'Shit sandwich.'"

—DIVINE SPREAD, HEAVY METAL HISTORIAN AND *SPINAL TAP* ENTHUSIAST

"Finally, an accurate artistic representation of the Bridal Industrial Complex. Bartness cleverly explores the deception and inherent greed therein. His tell-all confidential will expose some very important people of influence as the charlatans they are. Bartness is kicking ass and taking names."

—EMILY WENT, *THE WHIPPING POST*

Wedding Agenda

Ceremony Events ✓
- Pre-Wedding Music ✓
- Bridal Party ✓
- Bridal Processional
- Recessional

- Ceremony Starts 4:00 pm
- Arrive 2:30 pm

- Songs to Play

- Songs not to Play

Recpti

Ask about
extension
cords?

* Get confirmation
on Fireworks !!!

Re
Reception Agenda
1. Receiving Line
2. Couples Entrance
3. Open Buffet
* Best Man/Bridal Toast
5. Dinner Hour Music
6. Cake Cutting
7. 15 min break?
8. Bouquet Toss
9. Garter Removal/Toss
10. 1st Dance
11. Father/Daughter
12. Mother/Groom
* 13. Open Dancing
14. Send Off

HEY!

www.ingramcontent.com/pod-product-compliance
Lightning Source LLC
Chambersburg PA
CBHW060544160726
47991CB00001B/433